PLACE of SHELTER

To Pat Marek and Larry Berghoff,
who first read this novel;
to Toni Andrikopoulos,
the best listener a friend could have;
and to my brothers, Garland, Milton and Gerold

Place of Shelter

NOLAN DENNETT

NEW AMERICAN FICTION
SERIES: 30

LOS ANGELES
SUN & MOON PRESS
1994

Sun & Moon Press
A Program of The Contemporary Arts Educational Project, Inc.
a nonprofit corporation
6026 Wilshire Boulevard, Los Angeles, California 90036

This edition first published in cloth in 1994 by Sun & Moon Press
10 9 8 7 6 5 4 3 2
FIRST EDITION
©1994 by Nolan Dennett
Editorial Matter ©1994 by Sun & Moon Press
All rights reserved

This book was made possible, in part, through an operational grant from
the Andrew W. Mellon Foundation, through a grant from
The National Endowment for the Arts, a nonprofit corporation, and
through contributions to The Contemporary Arts Educational Project, Inc.,
a nonprofit corporation

Cover: *Farm in Northern Idaho*
Cover and Design: Katie Messborn
Typography: Jim Cook

LIBRARY OF CONGRESS CATALOGING IN PUBLICATION DATA
Dennett, Nolan
Place of Shelter / Nolan Dennett
p. cm — (New American Fiction Series: 30)
ISBN: 1-55713-130-9 : $19.95
I. Title. II. Series
PS3554.E53373P57   1994
813'.54—dc20
94-28963
CIP

Printed in the United States of America on acid-free paper.

PROLOGUE

THIS STORY I want to tell is part truth and part myth and part history. It's about my swinging wildly out from adolescence while growing up in Idaho. It's about some people I knew and some I dreamed about. It's an attempt to marry what was to the way I wanted things to be. A mixing of memories and desires to try and recapture the sense of astonishment and delight I knew as a kid. It's an attempt to light a candle in the darkness of half-remembered things, as I try to understand what happened and what didn't, and perhaps to answer the need I seem to have to name the names of those who came before me. The names of those who brought me here.

My story is set in central Idaho, with a cast of old movie types, like Errol Flynn and Lon Chaney. Set in the greens and browns and blues of the Salmon River region instead of the black and white of the silver screen. The Vinegar Man and Many Wounds, Cherokee Bob, English

Dan and Crazy Mary, Chinaman Sam and Polly are some of my characters.

And Jack Greegar and Corey.

I began telling my story to myself, before writing it down, walking in little circles in the center of my room, mixing up the truth with desires, memories with might-have-beens. Contemplating what happens to the little boys who have no one to teach them their prayers. Wondering, does the Sandman still lure them to sleep or is he martyred, shot in the back by their innocent neglect? Boys like Corey who grow up unloved and unwanted. Somehow perhaps, in the telling, I'll be able to bless the past with harmony and recapture that sense of magic and faith I felt the summer before I became a man. Magic and faith. Both can make something happen. Change what is impossible to change. I believe in both. I believe at times I had both.

I was born in Ontario, Oregon, the second son in a family of four boys. Soon after, we moved to Parma, Idaho, a small, poor town that owed any prosperity it claimed to the cultivation of sugar beets and the Parma Feed and Seed Company. My father was a small, handsome man who read cowboy books and dreamed of being tall. My mother and he were devout churchgoers and stood at the center of the Mormon Church in Parma. In southern Idaho you were either a Mormon or you weren't. As such they were intimately involved with church socials, Sunday school, and the daily pursuit of their faith.

My father, nearly illiterate, patiently bore his lot in life.

Which was always, until he died of cancer at the age of sixty-three, to work for other men. I can still see him clumping through the fields in his over-sized irrigation boots with a long-handled shovel over his shoulder. He had no vices, except for maybe ice cream. He was young until he was old, and then he died. I don't ever remember him having been middle-aged. His handsome, youthful face was always partly sunburned. I remember the feel of his big knotted fist around my hand. He was a man of few words. His callused hands told his story. He had two passions in life: baseball and dancing. My mother seemed to be happily involved in both. I say *seemed* because, of the two, she was by far the more complex.

There is no question that any perseverance I may possess was inherited from my father. Who, without a doubt, was the hardest-working man I ever knew. With his knotted hands and his back, he put four boys through college and two through missions for the church. In the course of my upbringing he moved the family from Oregon to Idaho to California and back to Idaho again. I remember we worked no less than six different farms in Parma the year before we moved to California.

We spent the spring of those early years in Idaho hoeing sugar beets and corn. In summers we bucked hay and harvested corn while Mom worked in the canneries. She would come home exhausted. Around the time the harvesting finished, Dad would start driving over to Ontario to work the swing shift in the Sugar Beet factory. Summer or winter, every morning and every evening, like clockwork, he would milk the cows. All of it—the planting, the harvesting, the cows, the work in the factory—was thankless, back-breaking work, and it never ended.

It was my mother who taught me to love art and books and music. She had a lovely alto voice and would sing in the church choir. Dad was tone deaf. This, however, did not keep him from swinging a baseball bat like a pro and dancing like Gene Kelly.

It is these two things then, dancing and baseball, that make up my earliest and fondest memories of childhood. Watching Dad play ball gave me an overwhelming urge to be a winner. Watching him dance with my mom gave me a love of beauty and theater that has never dimmed.

For some reason the memories of baseball come first.

The games would take place on weekends and would involve competitions between different congregations in the area called "wards." A group of wards in one region would make up a "stake." The regional winner would compete on a state level and so on and so forth. On the way to the game I would beg for money for crackerjacks. I would buy my treat, which would be gone all too soon, and then run up and down the bleachers delighted by the thunderous, irreverent sound my tennis shoes would make in the stands. The playing field seemed a magical place. The stadium lights were tall, elegant angels lifting aloft bright halos that would wink on at dusk and quickly fill with moths that swirled into the light like tiny graces dancing in a spotlight.

Under the bleachers was a dragon cave, a secret place, where I would hide and watch everyone gather, trying to guess who was who by the shoes they wore. The Wagstaffs, the Bowers, the Burgesses, the Reynolds, the Goats. I've forgotten many of the names now. I would feel something shift up above as I hid in my secret place, something in the energy of the crowd, and I would be drawn out of my labyrinth like a revenant to search for my mom in the stands. She would have brought a blanket to spread over our knees or shoulders to ward off the chill. We would cuddle up and the game would begin.

I have vivid memories of the sounds and the smells.

These are the most enduring: a ball stinging into a mitt, the crack of a bat when a ball was well hit, a grunt following a strike, cheers from the ladies in the stands, the shrill voices of the kids. The sound of these groans and cries and shouts was carried thinly out into the playing field in a way that I distinctly remember and can't quite describe. It was as if I observed from a distance, and it all took a slow-motion time to reach me. The sounds were coupled by smells of dust and sweat and leather, the blanket we huddled under, and my mom.

Then a batter would be hit by a wild pitch or an umpire would make a bad call and outraged insults would fly out of the mouths of the ordinarily serene ladies of the choir. Someone would slide for home. The game would go into overtime.

Dad would play shortstop or left field or catcher. As pitcher, the position he played most frequently, he was devastating—hurling strike after strike and throwing out unwary fools who tried to steal second. Bottom of the ninth he would get a hit. Sometimes I think he did it just to thrill us, our gladiator of the grass, our knight in knee pants and cleats. Without a doubt he was a hero. He didn't always win, but no one ever played harder or had more fun.

"Way ta go, Dad!"

"That's it, Lawrence."

Mom was the only person who called Dad by that name. Everyone else called him Dave. I know exactly how it sounded. Whether she was calling him in for supper or to come to bed. With the calling of his name and ours she wove a thread that made us family.

Throughout the game I would clutch a handful of gumdrops, saving the red ones until last. If I was lucky I would have a pocket full of change (full meant a quarter and a nickel) and go running for treats between innings—freezing Cokes swimming in buckets of ice or a hot dog that I would devour in two bites. It all flashes past like the wink of an angel. There would be a hayride through apple blossoms to begin the season, a harvest moon and a pit barbecue to finish it.

Once, after a game, our fat catcher, whose name I think was Mr. Anderson, took a dare that he could drink a gallon of A&W Root Beer in one breath. He had a formidable gut and would sweat like a hog throughout the game in his catcher's gear—at least a gallon. He hooked his middle finger through the handle of the jug, balanced the cold bottle on his forearm, tipped it up, and went at it. I watched in awe as the level of the root beer fell and his Adam's apple bobbled up and down. His big shiny face was topped by a bald head. The bottle seemed small in his grasp, but huge to me. We were all holding our breath.

I swear I could see his belly swell in direct relationship to the emptying of the jug. He almost made it, too, then dropped the bottle gasping to let loose with a belch of mythic proportions. Later he said he would have finished it all if he hadn't had to belch. Mom said he was just hoping to get a gallon of free root beer.

It was the last game of the season. Mr. Anderson did his dare with the melancholy sound of the emptying bleachers as a backdrop. I don't know if we won or lost. Someone said, "Great night for a game." My dad grinned with satisfaction. The dizzy sounds and smells of excitement faded as I fell asleep in the car on the way home.

∰

Sometimes it was just social, the dancing. Other times it was much more elaborate. Whatever, it was the one time work was forgotten, if only for a few hours.

Dad was handsome. Mom was beautiful. They were happy. The bands were local and probably not very good. There was always a waltz and a polka and a lot of fox trots. When the musicians were really daring they would try a tango or the cha-cha. It was the waltz, however, that was the best.

Dad would take Mom in his arms and the world would go away. In these moments there was only the two of them—no kids, no cows, no crops unplanted or unharvested. The church gymnasium became a ballroom. They floated. They flew. An angel stirred their waters and they entered the land of their dreams.

As I watched, I melted, and somewhere deep—on some profound level—I felt, even then, that if I danced I would be happy, too.

There was an annual spectacle called the Gold and Green Ball. A Queen of the Ball would be chosen from among the eligible debutantes and she would chose a consort. It was when Mom was Queen of the Ball that Dad fell in love with her I think. It was just before the war and

Mom had been dating Dad's brother Dean. Mom had broad shoulders, a full figure accented by a narrow waist. She looked smashing in the '40s fashions.

I imagine Uncle Dean watching them together with a look on his face like he'd swallowed a sharp blade. For their part they bore the expression of two parched hearts immersed in a long, cool, clear drink of water. Their thirst could be quenched only in each other. I imagine that Uncle Dean knew this even before they did. It was clear to anyone who watched them dance that they fit together like hand in glove. So Uncle Dean, gentleman that he was, bowed out and went away to war.

As I try to describe my parents and what they did for me I sometimes think they held me too close to be recognizable or that they are somehow too familiar to be known. In a way it's like trying to describe myself, and it's impossible to be objective. So, I don't know how, but I know what they gave me. The sense, the certainty that I could do or be anything. All was possible. The world was mine. They accomplished this in spite of themselves, because they certainly weren't perfect. But somehow they intimated without knowing, convinced without coaxing, so that I emerged from my adolescent struggles with my head up, unafraid. Without them the road would have been far more tortuous and obscure.

At night, before sleeping, I often close my eyes and call them up and try to lure them with me into dreams. Once there, I weave them into a sanctuary I can slip inside and be safe. With deepening breaths, I collect and count and

shape my memories of growing up in Idaho into cornerstones, walls, windows, and roof. Through years of green-
ing I have gathered materials for this place of shelter.
Mom and Dad, in my nightly constructions, are always
the cornerstones—the solid base I build my mansion
upon. The windows were put in place and opened by the
Vinegar Man, whose real name was Viktor. The Vinegar
Man gave me a point of view, windows through which to
see the world. Corey Greegar has come to be the landscape where I find my house of dreams. What passed
between Corey and me connects me to the past, defines
the present, and will always, inevitably, shape my future.

And so it is with meeting Corey that this story really
begins, when Dad moved us to another farm near a little
town called Warren in the Salmon River Region.

CHAPTER ONE

YOU USED to sit alone on the bus home from school. The big boys would pinch you, hard sometimes, if you had to pass them on the way to a seat in the back. Corey was the biggest and the meanest. Something in you, even then, told you he was mean because he couldn't get things right. In those days, maybe, it was his way of getting even. He still had power over you though. He tried to get you to show your dick to the other boys in the john during recess. You wouldn't and he laughed, then pulled his out and kneaded it a bit, like soft clay. You wouldn't look and left, followed by their snickers. Since you didn't pee at lunch you couldn't hold it and so asked to go in the afternoon class. You were always asking to go. The teacher, a new one, asked if there was something wrong down there, because you had to go so often. You said no, blushing with shame.

The teacher before this one was meaner and hadn't always let you go when you needed to. So one time, when you were younger, it leaked out and made a pool on the floor. You borrowed a friend's coat, because it was bigger and could hide the wet place down the front of your pants. You gave his coat back just before you got off the bus.

The teacher before this one had liked a round-faced boy with jug ears named Tommy the best and always let him lead the Pledge of Allegiance and held your paper up for ridicule because you drew pictures in the margins. You finished before everyone, always, and there was nothing to do. So you drew pictures. She didn't like it, so she held your picture up in front of the class and laughed. You stopped drawing pictures in the margins. This new teacher liked you better and Tommy wasn't the favorite anymore. You didn't know why. You acted just the same. It wasn't anything you did. Maybe because you didn't draw pictures in the margins anymore, but waited until you were home, in private, to draw.

The new teacher drank Lipton tea at lunch. You watched it steep. No one at home ever drank anything stronger than milk or juice. Sometimes vinegar and lemon with honey in it, but never tea or coffee. When she finished her tea we slid down the fire escape on the side of the lunch room to reach the playground. When we were good, that is. It always seemed our goodness was an arbitrary thing, more based on the mood of the teachers than the rightness of our actions.

During lunch, you sometimes saw Corey watching you, staring, but you didn't know what he was thinking. You wondered. Sometimes it made you afraid, sometimes not. Once he told you to look up one of the girl's dresses and you did. She got mad and ran to tell the principal. You got scared and hid in the bathroom. The principal came and got you out and made you sit in his room until lunch was over. He never said anything. You didn't tell him it was Corey's idea. Corey stood hidden at the side of the bathroom door when the principal came.

That day on the bus he pinched you again and you reacted, without thinking, slugging him hard on the shoulder. He laughed and pulled you up, flailing, when your punch knocked you off balance and onto the bus floor.

Sometimes Corey and his dad would work the other farms, helping weed sugar beets or de-tassel corn, depending on the crop and the season. Corey's dad had several teeth missing and smelled like a wine bottle that had been left lying too long in the sun. Corey never gave anyone trouble when he worked with his dad, but crouched in on himself, shoulders hunched up, and unsmiling. No stares now, but you would still catch him looking sideways at you when you tagged along, walking a corn row, following the harvesters.

Corey could work three rows, following the tractor wagon, ripping ripe ears off the stalks and tossing them into the back. You would trail behind, picking up strays. Corey never left many. He had big hands, no fingernails, and his arms were brown and dusty like the other men, even though he was still a boy not much older than you.

When Corey's dad, Jack Greegar, was around, Corey reminded you of a stray dog. One that has been kicked too many times and his mocking attitude toward you was masked, and you weren't afraid. Then you wanted to find excuses to bring him water and talk to him. Once, while he lay on the side of an irrigation ditch resting, with his head back and legs spread in the sun, he had you pour water from a canvas bag in his hair and down the front of his chest. He gasped and reached out to grab you, but you dropped the bag and ran. Later, you crept back and watched him sleep by the side of the ditch.

❀

You started having pains and your mom took you to the hospital with her. She had to have some tests, and so she took you in to have some, too. You can't remember the exact order of things.

They gave you medication and your eyes wouldn't focus, and so you couldn't read, which was bad. The doctor put on a rubber glove and felt around inside your bum hole, while your mom watched. He poked around and asked if there were any tender places. Stupid question. When you turned around to pull up your pants, there was a look of disgust and sympathy on your mother's face.

The doctor gave you shots. You got hepatitis. The pains didn't go away. So they decided to enlarge your bladder.

They stuck a needle with a little flat plate on the end of it up your penis, and used leverage to stretch your bladder wider.

In those days, I guess—I really don't know why for sure— they didn't anesthetize children, so I was awake for the entire operation.

You screamed and screamed until you passed out from the pain. They gave you a pill to sleep—afterward. The next day you woke up to hear another boy screaming the same way. He kept saying, "Let go of me, lady. Let go!" The nurse was holding him down. You heard the doctor tell your mother that his kidneys weren't working at all. You fell back asleep.

The next time you woke you told the nurse you wanted to visit your mom, who was staying down the hall. The nurse, a little fat Mexican lady, got you into a wheelchair and started to push you down the hall. It seemed funny to you. Your mom showed you a bottle with a narrow neck they wanted her to pee a sample into. You both laughed. Then you weren't feeling so good anymore, and so the nurse came to take you back. On the way you felt like you were going to throw up, so the nurse started to run, pushing you in front of her. You started to laugh and couldn't throw up.

Everything was funny that morning until you had to pee and then you wanted to scream again, but instead you just cried. The nurse caught you trying to climb back into bed. The pills they gave you made you dizzy and she had to help. She asked you what you were doing out of bed. You said, "Bathroom." She showed you the bedpan. No one had told you what it was for. No one had told you anything. It was quite a surprise when you discovered they intended to stick a needle up your penis and that you would be awake to watch them do it.

Finally they sent you home. Shortly after, you started peeing blood. Before you would urinate, you would be wracked by a spasm of pain, a convulsion you could control by clenching all the muscles in your stomach and turning your body into a fist. Finally you would weaken, and blood mixed with urine would leak out. When it got to be the spasms were pretty much constant, your dad said, "Let's go. We're going back to the hospital." The latest convulsion passed as you were going down the driveway. The relief was so great you started to quietly sing "Oh, Holy Night." Your favorite song.

When you got to the hospital, there was a young intern on duty. Dad told him about the spasms and the blood. The intern asked you where it hurt.

You said, "It doesn't right now."

He said, "Don't lie to me!"

His accusation shocked you into silence, and by the look on his face you knew he was going to do something horrible to you, because he thought you had lied to him.

That's why, I assume, they catheterized me.

There wasn't a nurse on duty, so the intern had your dad hold you down while he forced the rubber hose into your bladder by way of your penis. You screamed and wanted to kick the intern in the face as he worked between your legs, but maybe because your dad was holding you, you didn't. You passed out for a moment and woke to hear the intern telling your dad to sit down and put his head on his knees.

This time your stay in the hospital was longer, lasting through the spring and most of the summer. While you were away the family moved again to a farm closer to the river. Your dad had been taken on as hired hand. For the next two months you lived in terror of the same pain, when they would take the hose out. No one told you it would be like piddling. Hardly any pain at all. No one told you, and so you suffered in silence. Afraid to ask. Afraid to know. Afraid of what they were going to do to you next. After they put it in, your dad came back to the hospital the next day and patted you awkwardly and asked if there was anything the could get for you.

They had finished the last haying when you were well enough to leave the hospital and go home. The corn was finished and the summer gone with the hired hands.

I still remember my first impression of the new house, which is somehow wrapped up in the most recent. Ordinary, empty, but surprisingly disturbing. In the way a smiling man, who suddenly scowls and curses, is disturbing. Out of nowhere menace seemed to lurch into the air, stumbling into visibility, as I got out of the car. I remember even now how the goose-bumps puckered my flesh in the bright afternoon sun. As if I was surrounded by unromantic fog, or listening to music played slightly off key.

The discomfort was not apparent at first, but crept in slowly, blanketing the ordinary with a thin veneer of unex-plainable distress.

That first day back, you stood shivering in the front of the house for a moment after getting out of the car. A tire trailer sat in the driveway with the last of our shabby furniture. We hadn't been standing there long when the daughter of the landowner, last year's homecoming queen, pulled up to welcome us. She unloaded a few boxes. Having her there at that moment of vulnerability was embarrassing. You didn't know how to be warm to her and was glad when she left.

The house was brick with wooden floors, two stories. The bedrooms and a bath were upstairs. Kitchen, living room, and den downstairs, with another bathroom off the side of the kitchen—ordinary. When you sat on the downstairs toilet, you faced a door that led down some haphazard wooden steps to a cellar. There were a few shelves down there and a tank containing heating oil for the furnace. The bottom of the house was not flush with the top of the cellar walls so it was possible to see under the foundation of the house. It seemed somehow both dusty and damp down there.

For some reason you decided to turn this cellar into a studio. You had started turning your drawings into paintings, in those days just back from the hospital, and you fancied the isolation the cellar would afford. You rigged up a light bulb on a string and set up your oils.

After you got settled in, you would spend hours down there, able to tell where everyone was in the house from their hollow sounding footsteps on the wooden floors. The furnace, recently turned on to take the chill off the autumn nights, purred beside you.

Mom got a job working in a fish-fly-tying factory and started getting up very early to go to work. Soon you were in the habit of getting up just after she left and going down to paint for a while. You hadn't yet started back to school. You would hear your younger brother, Jerry, get up, run to the bathroom, then downstairs to curl up on the heating vent in the den, which lay directly over the cellar. He was ten years old that autumn. The baby of the family. You could hear him breathing right over you, panting, after his run down the stairs. He was always cold in that house and would sometimes crawl in bed with you at night to get warm.

You started a series of paintings that had a running figure in it. The figure wouldn't emerge. You didn't know if it was a woman or a man, but you did know it was running, pursued. You must have done ten versions of it.

Your little brother would whisper questions to you through the vent, pressing his face against the grill in the floor.

"What are you doing?"

"Painting."

"What?"

"Someone running. Down some stairs, or up."

"Is she scared?"

"Maybe."

"Does she have bad dreams?"

"I don't know, maybe."

His whispers filled the cellar as you sat under the naked light bulb and stared at your picture, seeing in your mind's eye what it was supposed to be, but unable to get your hand to bring it to life.

Sometimes you would lift weights down there while you waited, to try and get your strength back, your brother whispering while you strained below. After a while you would trudge heavy-footed up the stairs. He would wake up, startled, and run back upstairs to get dressed and outside to wait for his bus.

You still hadn't started back to school yet. It would be your first year of high school.

Jerry wouldn't stay in the house alone. Mom would find him sitting on the step outside when she came home in the afternoon. Once you started back to school you would leave him there in the morning.

One of your first times out and about, you and one of the dogs walked down the hill past the barn and toward the river. You didn't expect to go far. The dirt road curved through empty fields and you passed the cows walking themselves back to the barn for the evening milking. The air had turned away from summer and toward autumn. You saw what looked like Corey tilling a field in the distance. The smell of newly turned earth drifted toward you as you walked in the dust of the road. Ahead, two crows fought over a piece of glass. Trees gathered religiously on the banks of the river, ushering the water onto the next farm. Feeling tender toward all these things, you sat down when you got to the river and watched the water swirl away.

"You ain't brought me no water in a long time." He pitched a stone into the river, like he was mad. "I hear you been sick."

You started looking for a stone to pitch.

"I heard what they done to you." For a moment, curious. "You look skinny. You want a ride back on the tractor?"

He'd been in the sun all summer long and so he was more tan than ever. He looked strong and big as a man.

When you made a move to climb up in back he said, "Better get in the front."

You hesitated and so he added roughly, "I gotta go through the field and it's bumpy. I don't want you fallin' off on me."

Still you hesitated, unsure.

"Well? You comin' or not? In the seat."

You climbed up awkwardly, not wanting to appear weak. You were glad when he didn't offer any help, but you were nervous and sat gingerly on the edge of the seat. It felt close. He smelled warm. He put the tractor in gear and it lurched forward. The warmth from his thighs began to surround you, and for a moment you were frightened when he gripped you tight with his knees. You made a move to push him away, but then didn't. He seemed mad.

At the very last though, just as we pulled out of the bumpy field into the quiet of the road, I remember I felt safe.

As we came up the hill past the barn, Corey stiffened. His dad's pickup truck was parked by the side of our house.

Corey turned off the tractor and you started to climb down. Jack Greegar called over.

"You been loafin' around with this kid or you been workin'?"

Corey's face darkened, but he didn't say anything. He waited for you to get down, then stepped off himself.

"I ast you a question. Did you get the work done they been payin' you for?"

Jack Greegar took a pull off his bottle then hoisted himself out of the pickup. Corey stood waiting. You ran in the house. Mom had bread in the oven and the smell of it filled the house. You watched through the window. Jack pulled a long-handled shovel out of the truck.

You heard your mother running a bath upstairs. Corey hadn't moved. You watched Greegar's face contort as he hauled off and slapped the ground at Corey's feet with the shovel. Your mom climbed into the tub. Outside, Corey stamped down on the shovel handle. Jack tried to pull it out from under Corey's foot, but couldn't. He was too drunk, and probably not strong enough. Something had changed. Corey wasn't hunched in on himself, as he faced his father. His shoulders were down, his big chest was open, and his hands were fists at his side as he waited.

Greegar smashed his whiskey bottle on Corey's elbow, and then stopped to stare for a moment at the wet spot in the dusty road. Corey held his elbow, unflinching, and waited. The loss of whiskey took the fury out of the confrontation for Jack, but not for Corey, who still stood with his foot on the shovel handle. The bathtub was draining upstairs and your mother came down the stairs drying her hair.

"Is that Corey out there?"

Old man Greegar had driven off.

"Go ask him if he wants some hot bread."

You pretended not to hear, so she hollered out the window.

Corey didn't answer when your mom called, so she went out to him. You watched. They talked for a moment and then Mom took his arm and lead him gently up onto the porch. He sat and let her look at his elbow. She uncurled his fist and held it in her lap. She leaned in toward his head, which has bowed. You came outside and into the yard. Pressed up against a tree you watched them.

Words drifted out to you. Something bad. Something about Corey's big brother, John. You couldn't hear. Greegar drinking all night, every night. Corey saw the two of them and he knew why John left. Why he joined the Army. Why John hated him. Corey started to tremble. You inched closer.

You heard him say, "The same thing started again, with me. He keeps trying it with me, but I'm stronger now he can't force—"

Mom looked up and through the screen door, but her

eyes didn't register. She looked white. She put an arm around Corey's shoulders. You felt strange watching this. Corey's trembling stopped for a moment and then started again, until the two of them were shuddering there on the porch.

You ran onto the porch and the screen slammed behind you. Corey looked at you. You wanted to pull him away from your mom. You grabbed his bruised elbow. He flinched. Your mom covered your hand on his elbow with hers. It was cool and comforting, but you pulled away and thought of two years ago, last spring, when you slugged him on the bus.

Corey turned to your mom and finished saying, "He used to make John drink whiskey and then burned him with cigarettes until he took him into his room."

You recoil, shocked. Corey stood to shuffle his feet. Your mom's hands rested in her lap. Corey waited for a moment, like a hurt animal that is cornered and looking for an escape, then moved out the screen door and off the porch.

"I've got to take the tractor back down to the barn and get on with the milking."

You scrambled ahead of him to sit in the tractor seat.

"Git down from there!"

"No."

"Git, will ya please. You're pissin' me off."

You stared at each other. Finally, he swung up onto the seat behind you and shrugged his shoulders at your mom, who was standing holding the screen door open.

"Come back up for some supper. We got fresh, home-made bread. I'll tell Dad you're going to bunk out here for a while."

You took the tractor back down to the barn and then

watched while Corey set up for the milking. The cows had already walked themselves in and waited outside in the corral. Corey spread straw on the barn floor and hooked up the milkers. You heard your mom calling you in for supper. You asked Corey if he would come up, too. He didn't say anything, just plodded along with his chores. You stood for a moment watching him in silence. Your mom's voice came again in the distance, so you went out, leaving him putting oats in the stalls.

There was hot bread and chili to eat. Sitting at the big table in the kitchen, you kept thinking of Corey working silently in the barn and of his pa threatening him with the shovel.

The first day back at school, a couple of boys came up to you in study hall and introduced themselves. You felt frightened. You'd been away from school too long and felt like you didn't know anyone. You didn't know how to act. It mattered too much to you whether they liked you or not. So when they said smile and say hi to everyone and you will be fine, your face froze and you projected a fake sense of superiority that you did not feel. They turned away, faces suddenly cold.

That same week a good-looking girl named Rhonda transferred from a neighboring school. When she signed in, she turned down the passbook to the sports events, saying that she wouldn't be going, and if she did, it wouldn't be to cheer for her new school. The rivalry between the two schools was legendary. A girl named Lilly, assisting the registrar, overheard all of this and spread the word that the new girl was a stuck-up bitch.

That morning, not knowing any of this, you took your courage in hand, and as you waited for your first-period teacher, went over to introduce yourself to the new girl. At that precise moment the hall began to fill with angry friends of Lilly from the registrar's office. You were leaning against the wall, trying to be friendly, when they started muttering and then shouting things at Rhonda. At first you thought it was you. Then they started throwing things. A candy bar landed, smack, on top of the books Rhonda carried in her arms. Disdainfully, with the tips of her fingers, she picked it off and dropped it to the floor. You moved aside. She faced them alone, secure in her contempt for them. You were unable to watch, and left, flushing with shame.

You had started spending more and more time in your 'studio,' more and more time alone, hurrying home to continue work on your sketches and escape the torment you felt at school. You decided to expand the studio and so started to pull down the shelves that lined one wall. It turned out to be more of a job than you expected. Part of the wall came away, too. Dust filled the cellar. You started coughing. You couldn't see the other wall except for the dim outline of your running figure, a full-length sketch. But the head was at the wrong angle. She should be running toward you, not away. You pulled down the last shelf. A brass box, which had been behind it, fell to the ground spilling out a half dozen old keys. You seemed to hear a child cry out in its sleep. Your brother taking an afternoon nap in his room? It sounded as if he was weeping softly, perhaps disturbed by the noises from the basement. But he's not in his room, he's whispering overhead through the heating vent, "What do they open?" Then, "Don't open it, don't open it." Followed by the soft, sad weeping from upstairs.

You emerged like a ghost from the cellar, covered in dust, leaving the box and the keys where they had fallen. You find Jerry asleep on the heating vent, shivering. When you wake him, he turns his face to show scars from the vent temporarily burned into his face. For a moment you don't recognize him and you have the sensation you've stumbled upon a stranger in the house, but it feels as if you are the one who doesn't belong and the stranger has always been there in that room over the cellar, waiting.

🙟

That night I dreamed I was the one throwing candy bars at Rhonda and I laughed out loud in my sleep, delighted.

🙟

The next day, before Mom went to work and before you went down to the cellar to try and finish the remodeling you'd started, you told her you hated school and you didn't want to go back. Your rage seemed all out of proportion and didn't feel like your own.

That day at school you asked a girl—a blonde with curls and a womanly figure—if you could sketch her. She responded by loudly asking if you are queer. She'd said it as a joke, but you blushed to the roots of your hair and everyone laughed. Corey, loudest of all.

"Hey, Clinton, you wanna sketch mine?" He started to undo the buttons on his pants. As he did so, he walked slowly over to stand in front of you until his crotch was touching the edge of your desk. He hesitated, grinning at you suggestively. He looked down at your open sketchbook then back at you. "Naw, you don't have room on the paper."

"Go on, Corey, take it out. Maybe he can squeeze it in for you!" one of his buddies shouted.

"That's okay. I'd hate to be disappointed after going to the trouble of getting it all the way out."

Followed by snickers and whistles he turned back to his desk, swaying his narrow hips provocatively. Later he sat across from you in study hall and whispered secrets to his friends.

There came to be a weeping child in my dreams, a figment of my imagination that I at first mistook for my little brother, Jerry. Also in these night visions there was a Ghost of myself, not myself, coming up from the cellar, heavy-footed on the wooden stairs, but making no sound as it went to attend to the weeping child. But the door is locked. Someone wanted to keep him out. Rage filled the dream. The baby turned over to reveal a deformed head, and the Ghost wept, smiling malevolently.

You started over on your painting, making the changes you had seen in your dust-filled vision. The woman ran toward you now, no longer looking over her shoulder.

There was a feeling in the air that the long summer was finally coming to an end. The farmers were rushing to finish the last of the haymaking before the rain came and mildew set in. Corey had been staying in the loft above the barn for nearly a month now. Lately, on the weekends, he and your dad had been working across the valley, helping various neighbors buck hay. They worked from sunup to sundown lifting the eighty-pound bales onto a slip pulled through the alfalfa field. When the slip was full, they would take the load in and stack it, then back to the field to begin again. It was mindless, back-breaking work. But the weather was still holding and it was good to be out of doors. At noon, you and your mom took lunch to the men. Stronger now, you decided to stay and help with the afternoon work.

They made you do the hardest job, lifting the bales and tossing them to Corey, who was waiting on the slip. By late afternoon you were numb with fatigue and counted the remaining bales in the field. Corey jumped off and started to give you a hand. You had gotten too slow to keep up with the tractor.

A family of mice were exposed to the sun as you stood one of the last bales on end. You hadn't seen them and sat to rest for a moment on the overturned bale. Your arms were scratched, elbow to wrist. You had been too dumb to know better than to wear a short-sleeve shirt. Your hands had blistered, even through the gloves. They were so swollen you could hardly make a fist, let alone lift another bale of hay.

One of the mice ran up your baggy pant leg. You didn't know what it was. You just knew you had to get rid of it. You started dancing around the field trying to shake it out, to the vast amusement of Corey and the other hands. You ended up tearing open your pants. Your underwear had holes in it and your terrified weenie had shrunk to the size of a peanut.

"Good show, Clinton. I think you have a real career ahead of you." The crew boss was laughing so hard there were tears running down his face. "You and Corey put the tractor in the barn when you finish this last load. Unless you're planning to do an encore?"

He and the rest of the crew turned away, still chuckling and shaking their heads.

"You know, Clinton, for a smart guy you sure do some stupid things."

"Why don't you just shut up, Corey. I'm sick of you and I'm sick of being the butt of all your dirty, mean jokes." You were choking with embarrassment and on the verge of tears. "Just leave me alone!"

"Well, if I was going to strip naked in front of an audience I would at least make sure I had something to show."

"Oh, fuck you, Corey. Fuck you." You shoved past him to scramble up into the tractor seat, but slipped and smashed your shin, hard.

Then the tears did come, but you couldn't bear to let him see, so you slammed the tractor into gear. It jerked forward, knocking Corey off the slip and onto his butt, and then stalled. Suddenly things weren't so serious anymore.

"Hey, where'd you learn to drive, hotdog?"

"Where did you learn to walk?" But you both were smiling.

Corey brushed himself off, sheepishly, and climbed up next to you on the tractor seat.

"Try that," he said as he put it in first gear. "You might have better luck. At least if you want to go forward."

He rested his hand on your shoulder as you began to move across the field.

"Let's have a swim when we finish, okay?"

You hesitated for a moment before consenting. "All right, then."

The two of you unloaded the last slip, then ran to a big irrigation ditch down the hill, tearing off your clothes as you went, and jumped in. The evening air was still warm, and so, after splashing around a bit and washing off the dust of the field, we lay half-dressed on the grassy bank. There was a companionable silence for a moment and for the first time you felt almost comfortable being alone with Corey. Then out of nowhere he said, "It doesn't look so small now."

At the house, the farmer's wife gave you night clothes to change into. You were to spend the night and move on to the next field in the morning. She took the clothes from a chest at the foot of the bed. They smelled of cedar wood. You had no dreams of the weeping child that night, and our discarded work clothes filled the room with the scent of alfalfa.

CHAPTER TWO

H E'D COME twice in spring and twice in fall, usually when the haying was done. It was so that first fall you spent in the house. He'd come calling for *"Knives!"* from the housewives and *"Bottles!"* from kids. Twice in spring and twice in fall, asking for scissors to sharpen, searching for bottle caps for jugs. The King Lear of Sike-Sike, White Medicine Man from "Foot-of-the-Mountain."

"Wizard of Dreams!" he'd call. "Berries into Wine!" Sometimes the sing-song of "Vinegar, Vinegar, Vinegar Man!" came echoing back from kids doing hide-and-seek after him. You'd done it, too. They'd sneak up close, whispering, "He knows the bogey-man. The sandman, too."

"A dragonfly will sew up your lips if you tell a lie."

If they got too close, he'd stop his wagon, tugging his old nag to a halt. Then he'd rest motionless, for a moment. The kids would freeze. He'd turn slowly, then smile or wink, and finger to forehead, he'd come to some conclusion and dive into a gunny sack in the back of his wagon. They'd run off for a bit then, teasing and calling out to him, but always, eventually, coming back again, closer. Especially the little boys who had no one to comb their hair, hoping for a glimpse inside his gunny sacks, his jars, and his head. Sometimes he'd give you a ring or show you a curiosity in exchange for a bottle cap or a pair of dice. He'd come creaking and mumbling down the lane or through the middle of town. Once he explained to the barber's wife her dream. Other times he'd be seen following his cart down Main Street, slower and slower, until he nodded and blinked and winked and sailed off while standing right in the middle of the street, face back and up to the sun, asleep. Thawing his arthritis in spring, soaking up warmth for winter in fall.

"Fetch me your mom's scissors," he'd say and give you a berry as a bribe. "Tote those newspapers to the wagon. Yes?" When they'd hesitate he would say, "I know a berry patch where this is the smallest one," and he'd hand you a blackberry bigger than his gnarled old thumb.

Banging and clanging and stirring up dust, he'd chase the autumn away before him. Birds waited until the last minute to skip and dart and spitter away in front of him, to come circling overhead, riding his dust cloud of energy and noise, reeling from the smell of ripe fruit and sunlight wafting up to them, these aerial sentinels, riding his wake.

Banging and clanging he'd arrive.

"Time to clean the windows and air out mattresses. I saw the Vinegar Man in town today, sure sign of spring. Or they'll be picking apples soon, the Vinegar Man is back in fall."

Sure enough, a few weeks later, you saw him coming

down the lane. First you heard him. His melancholy tune drew you out from your reverie in front of your fleeing portrait in the cellar. "Wizard of Dreams. Berries into Wine. Vinegar, Vinegar, Vinegar Man." You came upstairs to watch from the window of your bedroom as he stopped to shuck and sample an ear of corn from the field on the North side of the lane, then cross over to the field of sugar beets to the South, tasting and measuring the sweetness on his tongue.

"Sweet!" He'd say. Or, "Not so."

And under your breath at the window, "Vinegar, Vinegar, Vinegar Man. Face me and chase me and catch me if you can."

He smacked his lips and smiled after sampling the crop, showing all his teeth, and then climbed back up onto his wagon seat, still smiling. Three crows circled overhead and a hummingbird dive-bombed in their midst, a friendly assault on the flowers in Posey the Nag's mane. He laughed, his teeth showing through his nest of whiskers like pearls. The sound of his laughter harmonized with his clanging pans and the wagon wheels' squeaks, and the jingle of Posey's worn-out harness.

The sound of Posey's clomping hooves, his bubbling laughter, and the wind sighing through the alfalfa field in front of him, where the lane curved; these sounds came skipping down the road to tap on the window of your room.

The house seemed to pause then in its dark machinations and listen. Seemed to turn and watch his approach. He, curiously, paused, too, and stood on his wagon seat at the curve in the lane. He raised his hand, a shaman's epitaph, as if in acknowledgment of the sinister attention paid him by the house. Then a cold wind began to stir in your sepulchral studio, and whined through the heating vent to rush up the stairs and into your room. A cold wind, which you could touch and almost see, not just feel, that raged about the room, gaining momentum, before it dove out the open window to stop short in front of the Vinegar Man's raised arm!

The birds hung suspended in the air now, motionless, wardens and witnesses with the Vinegar Man to the evil force from within the house. Adjuncts to the premonitory gesture of the Vinegar Man's raised hand, their presence seemed to keep the fetid vapor from traveling farther down the lane.

Slowly, as you whispered, "Wizard of Dreams," from where you watched, the Vinegar Man lowered his hand to a bundle of herbs tied at his waist. Then raising a clump of sage, he shook it three times into the wind. The crows struck the air with their wings in chorus of him. In response, the breath from the house seemed to shimmer and condense, and the hair on the back of your neck rose as if an icy finger were tickling you there.

Sweating, your heart beating wildly, you sank into a daydream spell of no thought and no emotion. A weightless sense of floating in a sea of iridescent air encompassed you and held you suspended there by the icy breath caressing your spine. Time stopped and the Vinegar Man truly became a Wizard of Dreams, Jeremiah commanding a Fallen Angel as he addressed the wind.

"You do not ride on the back of Metatron. His wings do not shelter your presence here. Gabriel's horn does not call you forth. You make Michael and the other archangels weep. You are not one of them. You do not stand before the face of God. Even this cherubim"—indicating the hovering hummingbird—"is greater than you. Be gone and trouble me no more." And he drew his arm to the Sign of the Square. "Be gone you toad, you gargoyle," he commanded. "You have no power here." And a third time, "Be gone!"

But the ghoul of air from the cellar hung there, unmoved.

At this precise moment, Jack Greegar's truck came bouncing over the railroad tracks and turned down the lane.

"Out of the way you old fart," Greegar shouted, sticking his head out the window of his cab.

Posey the Nag looked sideways, disdainfully.

With a flick of his fingers, the Vinegar Man called out a final incantation: "Metatron! Michael! Gabriel! Go!" and he directed the three crows into the shimmering wind in front of them. With a triumphant cawing, they dove, graciously, like doves, into the whirlwind. There was a flash of sunlight on their wings and a flurry of feathers. The dust devil began to disperse, then gathered itself again to rush after Greegar's truck, where it snatched the hat from his head. But he grabbed it back and crowned himself with the center part of the maelstrom from the cellar.

"He has named his name," remarked the Vinegar Man, and the spell was broken.

You moved downstairs and outside now, wondering, and the Vinegar Man answered, without your asking.

"Your dreams will change now. Your Ghost will have an identity and you may learn to protect yourself and find who you are." He handed you the bouquet of dried sage. "Burn this and let the smoke drift into the four corners of your room. It will help you be safe."

He held your hand for a moment as you took the sage, and his warmth poured into you. His eyes twinkled and flashed at the crows, who came swooping down to weave a web of magic around you.

Jack Greegar was on his way to the river road and Rivertown when he passed through and became possessed of the dust devil from the house. He had two ideas in mind. One was to finish his whiskey, the other was to get laid. His teeth were grinding badly, and he itched all over. He hadn't had enough to drink, and so took a swig from the open bottle on the seat beside him as he passed the Vinegar Man's tired old wagon and nag. The whiskey rushed like a bolt of lightning to his brain. The road blurred for a second and the river bottom in front of him changed colors. The wind nearly snatched away his hat, and as he furiously clamped it back down on his head, a thousand piercing maniacal voices seemed to penetrate his skull and take up residence there, turning the horizon red. He obviously still hadn't had enough to drink. He was starting to be able to smell himself.

There was a direct connection between Greegar's cock and his brain. When one was awake, the other was awake, and the lower was always the more awake of the two. Greegar had never understood things. He'd never understood what other people feel and why they took care of each other. He'd never understood that dreams are not just for those who sleep. In fact, he never understood much of anything, except how to satisfy his appetites—eating, drinking, and getting laid. He was a lanky, big-boned man, but not fat, and it sometimes seemed his capacity for getting his appetites taken care of was endless.

When he was younger he had had a certain animal attractiveness to him. In those days he had been strong and singleminded, but his power had twisted in on itself, and so now, like a rabid dog, Greegar was running loose, ready to turn and bite for the simple pleasure of feeling his teeth sinking through flesh. Unlike a mad animal that will release its victim after a time, Greegar could pleasure himself endlessly with the struggles from the objects of his desires. For one of his victims to escape his tormenting before he was through was maddening to him. Thus his obsession with Corey.

Jack had almost convinced Corey his outlook was the real one—not by anything he said, but by his actions. Jack once tore a puppy to shreds with his bare hands because it piddled on the floor in front of him. He laughed the whole time, especially when Evaline had told him he had the mentality of a deviate.

"Ya, I got a mentality, and I've got something else you like, too."

He'd met Evaline fifteen years before, when he was still holding down a job driving truck. One night he was horny as hell, so he got on the CB and did a little advertising.

"I've got twelve long, hard ones and they call me Jack Hammer. Anyone out there got a tape measure?"

Evaline had taken the bait. They had rendezvoused at the Flame Motel just outside Burley, Idaho, and Evaline had been on her back for three days.

She'd been leaning on the hood of her Pontiac waiting, like she said she would, when Jack drove up. He flashed his lights and turned in across from her. He sat there in the dark of his cab, toying with her, as he lit and smoked a cigarette. All she could see, by the glow of the butt, was a glimpse of his long, hollow-eyed face. Finally, taking his time, Jack unzipped his pants as he stepped out of the semi, and slowly pulled it out to show her in the flash of the neon motel sign. The sign flashed and she glimpsed it swaying long between his legs. There was another flash and two larger than humanly possible balls joined it there. Flash, flash, and it rose to jut straight out. Again a flash and it touched the sky above his belly button, where he'd pulled open his shirt. His towering erection now matched in magnitude the inhuman aspect of his nuts. All this without touching it. By the third flash, Evaline was strolling over for a closer look, saying, "My, my, my, my!" all the way. All this in plain sight of the freeway.

Evaline didn't mind Jack's kinkiness at first. Later on she realized that a switchblade had left a mean streak on Greegar's soul that was deep and permanent. It was a pity. They had had a good time for a while. An erotic time was not enough for Jack, as she soon found out, but fascination with his monument kept her around long enough to produce Corey and his big brother, John. Evaline had lasted longer with him than anyone. She put up with a lot for the feel of his thing hard inside of her. When she caught him teaching seven-year-old John how to give him head, she left.

She had never considered the boys any part of herself, but figments of her unnatural desire for Jack. They had nothing to do with her. Especially as she considered they would end up being just like him anyway. And what would she do with two half-grown Jack Hammer's?

When Jack found her packing and asked where she

was going, she said, "I got me a train ticket to Hades. It has to be sweeter than this."

❀

The river road, where Greegar was headed, led to a hobo camp referred to as Rivertown. It was a collection of shacks and campsites that would come and go from year to year. The one permanent structure was a cabin built by the Vinegar Man years ago. This shantytown was inhabited, like all places of its kind, by an assortment of derelicts, whores, philosophers, and saints. The line between types was thin. The whore had the face of a saint and the philosopher easily turned derelict when his wisdom was blurred by drink. All were welcome at Rivertown—no judgment passed. A token of whiskey or conversation was appreciated, but not expected. A string of catfish for the community pot or another hand for the ongoing poker game was rarely turned down.

The Vinegar Man made his wine there. He'd collect fruit and berries to be found growing in the woods along the riverbank, mixing them with the other necessary ingredients and then storing it all in large plastic tubs to ferment. The result would be strained through a cheesecloth and stored or sampled, depending on the day or the mood of the brewer. If he sampled earlier efforts too often, the new batch sometimes would end as vinegar instead of wine.

Some days would be solely for sampling and his mystic musings would turn incoherent and his rambling conversations would involve another time, another place, another life, when he was young and answered to the name Viktor.

On those occasions he would lose his twinkle and himself in dark pools, and everyone knew it was best to just leave him alone. The only poultice for his delirium was Mary, who would lead him home if he wandered away and make sure Posey got bedded down properly.

Crazy Mary—the only one who would call him Viktor. The only one he would allow. Sometimes he would mistakenly call her Melissa and ask for a song. She would oblige with a lullaby or a nursery song. Simple things, often tuneless, but he would appear satisfied, at least for a time. His troubled brow would soften then and he would sleep.

She had all the sweetest stuff imaginable, Mary did. White skin and a baby face, all wrapped up in a porcelain body. She had a womanly figure, and all the know-how necessary to please any man, but she was missing something upstairs, and so she gave it away when she could have made a living of it. Now, from giving it away too often, she was missing a couple of teeth. She used to stay in town, spending most of her days looking at herself in the window of the barber shop or talking to the freshly shaved men, while she lounged under the big pear tree in the empty lot next door. Some of the conversations led to other things. Mary seemed to expect it, and would even encourage it sometimes by asking if they wanted to see her underwear. After a while she seemed to go off the deep end.

Mary's mama had rented the room above the barber shop and had worked in the saloon next door. Something had happened to her, though, before Mary was born, and so she rarely spoke, except in monosyllables, enough to get her work done. A pretty woman, she had an arrangement with the barber, whose shop she would clean in the mornings in exchange for him keeping an eye on Mary in the afternoons when she worked the saloon. Finally she just faded away. Died one night in her sleep. Mary, a teenager by now, took over cleaning the barber shop and shared the room upstairs with any tenant the barber could find.

He was the first, the barber, taking her one morning in one of his chairs when his wife was off visiting relatives in Lewiston. So Mary hung around, having nowhere else to go, and the barber would tell an admiring customer, "Go ask her if she's got pretty underwear." They would leave a big tip, clean-shaved and well-satisfied.

Well, word got around, and at some point along the line Mary's sweetness got spread too thin. A couple of out-of-towners got rough and she lost her underwear in the bushes out back of the pear tree. While she tried to find them, it started to rain. The Vinegar Man found her squatting in the rain-filled gutter in front of the long-closed barber shop, trying to wash the blood from between her legs.

He gave her a pair of dry pants to wear and she helped him lead Posey home. After that, she stayed at the river huts and helped the Vinegar Man make his wine. But she still had that sweetness that brings out the worst in some men and they would come to find her. Sometimes they would have to get by the Vinegar Man first, and sometimes he was too drunk to care, fighting off his dark swans with theurgical incantations and mystical names.

Mary, however, was not entirely helpless. After her episode with the out-of-towners behind the pear tree, some instinct took over and compelled her to discriminate in her choices. Whatever the instinct was, it had always kept her from accommodating Greegar, who had been sniffing around her ever since she moved out to Rivertown. When she wasn't interested she had an infuriating habit, at least to Greegar, of beginning to sing nursery rhymes. "Mary had a little lamb . . ." or "Ring around a— . . . baa baa black sheep have you any wool. London Bridge is falling . . . " and she would pet herself fondly between the legs. But she wouldn't open them for anyone. Sometimes this instinct for self-preservation could be overcome with whiskey. A ploy Greegar had tried on more than one occasion. One that he intended to try this night as well.

It was dark by the time Greegar reached Rivertown. He parked his pickup in a stand of cottonwoods not far from camp. Mary saw him coming and would have none of him, refusing his whiskey and his advances, pointed and vulgar. So Greegar was restricted to cheating Mannie and Joe at cards and continuing to get intimate with his bottle of Jim Bean. The voices in his head, undulled by drink, chattered and gnawed at him. His head hovered like a carnival mask on a pole in the campfire light, house for the evil vapor that had begun to have a life of its own.

🦢

You held the sage in both hands and watched as the Vinegar Man followed after Greegar's cloud of dust—a shining light on the tail of a dark vortex. The crows circled overhead protectively, while the hummingbird dove to ascend, dove to ascend, clearing the way into the approaching night. Not until they disappeared into the trees lining the river road did you leave your vigilant stance at the back of the house. You then trudged upstairs and placed your bouquet on the stand next to the bed. You took up your sketch pad and, with your left hand, for some reason, began to draw.

There you spent the evening, gazing out the window toward the barn, filling page after page with strange, convoluted figures. Now a woman, now a man. Unable to stop, your hand kept working even as you took your eyes away from the paper and looked about the room in a dreamlike stupor. You sketched and listened to the settling of the house, entranced. You felt yourself enter into a twisting passage, a fearful route of space and time, and you shielded yourself from dread by sideward glances at the clump of sage, pungent, on your bedstand. You fell asleep without knowing it. Your hand drew on.

In a dream the Ghost visited me again. Now with Greegar's face. Mom and Dad argue violently in the dream, something they never do. I'm painting in the cellar and Dad comes down with his boss, the landlord. Later I hear him telling Mom that she shouldn't let me work down there. He seems strangely adamant about it. I hide the keys I've found. Jerry won't sleep alone anymore. The Ghost with Greegar's face sits on the edge of my bed. I feel his weight.

You wake and he is gone.

I sleep again and he returns to tell me the baby was his sister's, and he sits on the window ledge rocking an imaginary cradle. He smiles and the rocking becomes violent. He tells me the baby is his. I hear steps running up the stairs from the cellar, but they come no closer. I hear weeping in the distance, now louder, now soft. Then silence.

You wake and the door knob to your room is slowly turning. Trembling and sweating, the reassuring sound of Corey finishing up the milking comes to you through the open window and the feeling lingering from the dream is arrested. You stand at the window to see light spilling from the open barn door. Corey's shadow passes through the light and back again, interrupting the light and throwing a long finger of a shadow up the hill toward where you stand at the window, watching. Freckles barks. The milk cans ring hollowly when struck together, answered by the tenor rattling of a pail handle. Mom calls from the foot of the stairs, a door opens, another closes. Water runs in the kitchen sink downstairs. Corey follows his shadow up the hill to place a pail of milk on the kitchen steps, then back down again to toss soggy filters to the waiting cats. You turn from the window, pick up the sage, and go to curl around the moonlight glittering on your waiting bed.

But sleep had been frightened away and would not return. You pulled on tennis shoes and, still carrying the sage, crept quietly downstairs and outside.

From the darkness you watched him. He'd come to be a permanent fixture, handling most of the chores now that your dad was working the swing shift in the sugar-beet factory in Grangeville. Sometimes he would join you and Jerry and Mom at the dinner table, sometimes not. He was always civil and silent around the house, at school derisive and sneering. He seemed to come closest to himself away from school and people, when working alone or exploring down along the river. You came to be a barometer for his moods, avoiding him at school, finding ways to follow along when you saw him out-of-doors, drawn to him then, the way water is drawn to the moon.

47

One Sunday, your mom talked him into coming to church. She lent him some of your dad's sabbath habiliments, and when he emerged from his loft and came up the hill, shy and disconcerted by the clean, dress-up clothes, you hardly recognized him.

"Gracious child! You look like a grown man and somebody important."

Your Mom had a lovely way of knowing just how to make a person feel good. With his hair slicked back and his face freshly washed, he was almost painfully handsome. Your mouth hung open at the transformation. This couldn't be the home-spun delinquent who, a few days before, had dragged you away from the drinking fountain at school to make room for himself and a bunch of giggling girls. He stared daggers at you now, daring some remark.

"Close your mouth, Clinton, you'll catch a fly. Now don't you worry, Corey. You look mighty fine. Everyone needs to go to church once in a while. Just follow along with Clint and do what he does. You'll be fine."

The usual greetings preceded our entrance into the chapel.

"Welcome to church, Myra. How are you, Clinton? Fully recovered, I hope? My, we didn't see you for the longest time. I see you have your scriptures with you this morning, good, good. And who is this fine-looking young man?"

Corey jammed his hands into his pockets and grinned at this attention from Betty Hill, who, in spite of her plump sensuality, was the most religious person in town. She had to be. Betty and Wayne Hill had eleven children and religion was the only thing that saved them from starvation and spiritual impoverishment.

Your mom rested her hand lightly on his shoulder as she said, "This is Corey Greegar. He's helping us out while Lawrence is working the swing shift in Grangeville. How are the little ones, Betty?"

The youngest, a thumb-sucking, tow-headed three-year-old, was clinging to her skirts. "Fine, fine. For whosoever drinketh of the water he shall give him shall never thirst. My meat is to do the will of him that sent me."

She referred to the fact that last payday they had done their usual monthly shopping, which had to be a momentous event with eleven children to feed, and, after packing their stationwagon full of grocery bags, had run back inside for some forgotten item, leaving the car unlocked and unattended. Well, someone helped themselves to everything, a three-month supply of food for an ordinary family. Betty had returned to find an empty car. She was so upset that she promptly collapsed onto the curb with morning sickness. She was expecting her twelfth.

The whole congregation had helped out, taking turns having the family over for the evening meal, or dropping off fresh bread, vegetables, and fruit in the mornings. Rumor had it that their kids had no manners and inviting them to dinner was an invitation to chaos. The kids ate with their hands and threw food at each other for entertainment when they were finished. Wayne and Betty smiled through it all, oblivious. Maybe they figured the Lord would provide discipline as well as nourishment.

"Plain stupidity," your dad said, and instructed Mom to send supplies. We would forego extending any dinner invitation.

Your favorite part of going to church was the organ

music, played by fat Mrs. Burgess or her equally fat daughter. They were into it, having an extensive repertory of Bach songs. Corseted and coiffed, with their pudgy feet strapped into high-heeled shoes, they nodded and smiled and marched up the aisle as we took our seats. They plopped themselves down and began to play an energetic duet. They jiggled when they played.

Corey seemed to be taking his first religious encounter entirely too seriously. So secure in your larger experience, you gave him an elbow to the ribs. "Check out the musicians." Nodding and smiling and jiggling, like two animated and overstuffed sausages, they began to butcher one of Bach's "Goldberg Variations" with the Mrs. playing and the daughter turning the pages with a triumphant flourish. Corey stifled a snort.

Shortly thereafter the musical prelude finished, and the meeting proceeded into opening prayer and opening hymn, then into announcements and the passing of the sacrament.

"Oh God, the Eternal Father, we ask Thee, in the name of Thy Son, to bless and sanctify this bread to the souls of all those who partake of it . . . "

In silence, aisle by aisle, the deacons passed the bread and then the water. In silence, they gathered at the back of the congregation when they finished. Solemnly, reverently, they collected the trays and returned to the sacrament table to offer the priests their turn at taking the sacrament. After partaking, the priests sat back down. The supplicants stirred and coughed as hymnals were pulled open once again.

"Oh, that I were an angel and could speak with the trump of mine heart!" rose to the furthermost corners of the chapel.

Corey sat quietly throughout this part of the meeting with his brown hands resting quietly on his knees, motionless except for his fingers curling and uncurling, caressing the unfamiliar fabric of his borrowed Sunday clothes.

There was to be a healing that Sunday, so when the hymn was finished a hush fell on the congregation again, some took hands, others embraced, and an old woman who had suffered a stroke was wheeled up to the pulpit. The left side of her face was frozen in a grimace, the right trembled and wept. Three elders of the church anointed her with consecrated oil and then laid their hands upon her head. At first, the blessing, spoken by the center of the three elders, was too intimate to be heard, but then, as he continued, he seemed to expand into his power and authority and it seemed that the spirit of the Lord was upon him.

"Now, Lucille, I bless you with every blessing that is in my power to do so at this time—with the health you require, with strength, and the desire to serve the Lord and keep his commandments, and I seal you up against the power of the adversary, until the morning of the resurrection when you shall come forth clothed in the Robes of Celestial Glory, to rule as a queen and priestess in the House of Israel and hand in hand with your companion, to enjoy eternal life in the presence of the Father and the Son forever. And I do this contingent upon your continued faithfulness, in the name of the Redeemer of Israel, Jesus Christ. Amen."

And the laity answered, "Amen!" and "Amen!"

On the way home in the car, Corey asked, "The woman in the wheelchair. Will she be healed?"

Mom answered, "You never know. It sounded to me like they were giving her permission to go and join her husband. He passed away almost ten years ago. She never remarried. Although at one time she was considered a beautiful woman. She thought it was adultery. She once told me, 'One man and one man only—for life.' Well, she stuck to that, and maybe now it's time for her to go and rejoin him."

There seemed to be an uneasy understanding between Corey and you that day. During the healing, when the congregation took occasion to lay hands on each other, your mom had placed her hand on the back of your bowed head and automatically, without thinking, you had put your hand over Corey's hand. For a moment he went rigid, then he relaxed and his thumb crept around two of your fingers and stayed there.

At Sunday dinner he watched you with an unfathomable look on his face. As if there was something he wanted to ask, but couldn't or wouldn't—some secret he felt you had that he must know. When you caught him staring at you he dropped his face to his food and didn't look up for the rest of the meal.

And now with the clump of sage in hand, like a moth to a flame, you'd come down from your room to sit in the dark and watch him finishing his work in the barn. You felt like a tide drawn to the gigantic moon just beginning to rise behind the barn. Was it the moon keeping you awake, drawing you outside, or was it Corey? You didn't know, and maybe it didn't matter.

By the light of a lantern, you could see him sitting on a bale of hay with his chin in his hands and his elbows on his knees. After a moment, he got up and started to climb into the loft and his bed roll. He laid out blankets and undressed. His neck, the front of his chest, and arms were brown from working in the sun. The rest of his body was pale by comparison. He started to stretch out, then realized he'd left the lantern downstairs. Naked, he moved to the ladder, his dick swaying gently between his legs. You could see it even when he turned his back to climb down the ladder. He bent to take the lantern and saw a pail full of milk. He picked it up to bring it outside and empty it into one of the big cans in the cooler. The light of the lantern was warm at his back, and the cool light of the full moon anointed him with a halo as he came outside, casting his face in shadows, so you couldn't read his expression when he saw you and stopped.

He was beautiful in the moonlight, as natural in his nakedness as the straw in the loft of the barn or the moon-lit hills covered with evergreens beyond the river. The plaintive anthem of some nestling night bird floated across the way, entrancing you. Were you asleep or was this a waking dream?

Finally, Corey spoke.

"What are you doing out here?"

"Nothing."

He didn't say anything else, so you added, "I couldn't sleep. Maybe it's the full moon."

"Ya, maybe it's the moon."

He moved on toward the milk cooler. As he emptied the pail, we heard a truck bouncing down the gutted road, up from Rivertown. Startled, Corey raised his head to listen. The headlights from Greegar's truck stabbed their way through the fields toward us.

You stood up, wiping the seat of your pants, and stumbled the rest of the way down the hill toward the barn.

Corey had turned into granite. You took the empty milk pail out of his hand and tried to push him toward the ladder to the loft. He wouldn't move.

"Corey—Corey, come on!" His stomach was warm beneath your hand. "Don't talk to him. Come on!" The pickup was getting closer. "Come on, now!"

You took his hand and tried to pull at him. The muscles in his neck and shoulders had tensed into knots.

The pick-up lights went out and the engine turned off, but the truck continued rolling, crunching gravel in the darkness as Greegar came on, like a nightmare, slowly and steadily down the lane toward the barn. Finally the truck stopped rolling and then . . . nothing.

You ran and blew out the lantern and ran back to shove Corey into the corner behind the milk cooler and then stood in the front of him in the shadow. A swallow guarding a sparrow-hawk. Through your T-shirt you felt him, warm at the small of your back. Then he covered himself with one of his hands and pulled you further into the shadows with the other. You caught your breath and held it, listening.

The pickup door opened. Greegar stepped out. We could hear his boots crunching gravel in the driveway. He flicked his lighter on and off and on. He moved away from the cab of the truck, then paused at the top of the rise, his silhouette twisted against the sky. He flicked his lighter on and off and for a moment we saw his mouth grinding in the light.

"Corey, you there, boy?"

Had he seen us?

"I got somethin' for you, boy." Flick-flick went the lighter. "I been wonderin' where you is. Where is you?"

Slowly, steadily, he came down the drive. Flick-flick, a slow-motion dream coming toward us, chewing his words under his breath, teeth grinding in the night. His face was distorted and he was swinging his usual whiskey bottle in one hand and carrying his lighter, menacing, in the other. His evil smell preceded him down the drive, brought to us by the night breeze.

One of the horses in the pen next to the barn snorted and distracted Greegar. He went to the fence, passing within three feet of us, hidden behind the cooler.

"You out there, boy? Ya, I got somethin' for you. Heh, heh, heh," he laughed, and unzipped his pants and started to piss in the dirt. Flick went the lighter, as he admired his dick while he pissed. Then to your surprise, he started playing with it. It was long, like Corey's, and started to get thick and stand up. You'd played with yours before, but you'd never seen a grown man do it. He stopped after a moment, though, and stuffed it back into his pants. He was standing close enough still so that the smell of his unwashed body and the booze and the piss on the ground was overpowering. He started mumbling for Corey again. His teeth grinding and his face twisting and going slack, while he flicked his lighter on and off and on.

There began to be a heat coming off of Corey's body to yours and you tried to melt further back into the shadows, afraid the warmth from the two of you would draw Greegar's attention. As if he were a beast of prey and your warm scent would draw him to you. You began to tremble in spite of the warmth. Corey responded by hugging you close to him with an arm around your chest. He did not seem frightened, tense; rather, a watch spring wound too tight.

Greegar stood mumbling at the fence. The demon voices in his head, rising, now falling, now rising. A cacophony of demented angels, a discordant choir, urging him, goading him, until now, fueled by drink, they had been growing louder and louder, more and more insistent, licking the open wound on his soul, deliciously tormenting him into becoming the beast of prey he already nearly was—some caged and primordial monster, rattling its chains, clamoring to be out!

Now, as we watched, a dark water of the air began to creep down the hill from the house like a disease to gather at Greegar's feet. It crept and curled around his skeletal legs, lingering in his crotch before oozing up his back and around his scraggy neck to caress his pale and cadaverous face.

He'd had no surcease for his perverse desires, no John, no Mary, and no Corey. So that now his body, like a festering boil, was demanding release. His voices whispered and chattered, goading him onward.

The sight of his gaping mouth and grinding teeth—his skeletal figure attended by mist—turned your blood cold and the hair rose on the back of your necks.

The horses, catching his scent, became agitated. Tossing their heads and snorting, they began to trot nervously back and forth, back and forth, in the corral. By the murky light of the no longer benevolent moon, Greegar looked slowly to the left and then slowly to the right, and his shadow lengthened toward where we cowered, frozen, in the darkness.

And now the mist began to take on a life and shape of its own, a dark dream with animated and darkly wrought features. This parasitic wraith appeared to exist half inside

Greegar and half independently, mirroring his movements, only slightly later, so that when Greegar turned his face in your direction, it turned, too, a heartbeat after. Turned to reveal the face of the malevolently smiling Ghost from your nightmare. Smiling, smiling, this Gemini of malicious intent began to execute a bizarre and disjointed duet with itself. Partnering him from behind, in some mythic and demented waltz, the Ghost caressed then slowly raised Greegar's arm. And a hook or some razor seemed to glitter there, and together, the Ghost and Greegar, brought it slashing down to point directly at us.

Hunchbacked by this Ghost, he didn't really see us, but somehow he knew we were there. When he spoke, his voice was like a winter wind. "Git out here, boy. I know where you are. I got what you want."

And the apparition began to draw Greegar to where we hid. Slowly, slowly, it oozed through him and forward. Then waited for him to catch up, as if his own shadow had stood up and become his pilot and was leading the way step by step toward us. He came on, sometimes seeming to enter a shroud, at other times carrying the whispering corpse on his shoulder.

Still hidden, Corey bent to gather a handful of gravel, then urgently whispered, "Run when I throw this!" He then stepped out from behind the cooler where Greegar could see him. You stepped to the other side and Greegar stopped short to look from one to the other of us.

Sneering, he said, "I see you been playing with each other's dicks."

At this accusation you flushed and looked quickly at Corey who blinked but did not take his eyes off of Greegar.

A bloody-black sack began to bulge in Greegar's brain upon seeing Corey naked there, bloody-black and ready to burst so all his pent-up vituperation could run free.

"Did you save some for your old man? Huh? Did you, boy? Did you?"

Corey began to inch sideways, widening the gap between the two of us. "I ain't got nothin' for you!"

"Is that so? You know I told you not to be givin' it away 'til I told you boy. You been giving it away to somebody besides me? Huh? I ain't through with you yet."

"I got news for you."

"Ya? What news is that?"

"Like I said, I got nothing for you. Now or ever again."

"Is that so? Maybe your little friend can help you change your mind."

In two long, swift steps he was on top of you, bringing his sepulchral scent with him. In another swift move he had his fingers around your throat and he'd shoved you up against the side of the barn.

"Now let's see what my boy's been after." The glittering razor he had seemed to hold was once more his lighter held level with your belt buckle.

"Take it out."

"What?"

"Don't mess with me, boy," he hissed. "Take it out."

He began to giggle and the night mist condensed and swirled around us and his strangle hold on your throat tightened, nearly lifting you off the ground. Still holding the clump of sage in one hand, you struggled vainly to get his fingers away from your neck, then froze, terrified as he began to flick his lighter with its enormous flame on and off in front of your crotch.

"Drop your pants, son."

"No!"

"Drop 'em. I'd hate to burn somethin' by accident." Greegar's Ghost seemed to nod its approval, hovering in the air over his shoulder.

"Okay, okay."

You fumbled with your belt buckle, still holding the sage, nearly unconscious from having to breath Greegar's rotten smell. You gingerly pulled down your pants. Greedily, he dropped his lighter and reached inside your shorts and up between your legs to squeeze your butt. First one side and then the other.

"Don't please!"

His hungry touch, embarrassingly, caused your dick to stand to attention and you tried to cover yourself. He knocked your hand away and pushed you hard up against the barn and down until you were sitting on his forearm while his long icy fingers continued to knead your butt.

Now he began to lift you on his forearm, sliding you up the barn wall, as he gazed eagerly at your jutting dick rubbing against his forearm. Staring, he turned his head from side to side, as if entranced by what he saw before him.

"Um, just enough for a little snack," and he began to giggle again in delight, and his spectral host seemed to echo back his pleasure with silent laughter of its own. Its gaping mouth opened and closed next to Greegar's ear.

Meanwhile, Corey had gathered another handful of stones and just as Greegar bent to take you in his mouth, Corey drew back and launched a handful of stones full force at his backside.

"Pick on someone your own size, asshole."

Enraged Greegar released you and turned snarling to face his son.

"Try that again, you little son of a—"

"Okay!" and hard on came another handful of stones.

Suddenly out of nowhere came a voice in your head. "Light the sage." So as Greegar lurched toward Corey, who was now scrambling up into the loft for his pants, you bent and picked up Greegar's discarded lighter.

Time now seemed to enter a dreamscape, where you run and run and run, but get nowhere. Slowly you brought the lighter toward the sage. Slowly you watched Corey, swimming through molasses as he fumbled to pull on his pants in the loft. Slowly you watched Greegar oozing up the ladder shrouded in his mist. And the voice, a record running at 33⅓ rpm's, repeated in basso profundo, "Light the sage. Light the sage."

One heavy foot after another, you ran in slow motion to the bottom of the ladder. Greegar was caught on its rungs between Corey and you, like a baboon on stilts— caught but not trapped. He shouted imprecations and abuse while snatching at Corey's legs. But Corey held the top of the ladder out from the edge of the loft and danced away from the clawing fingers. Momentarily outdone by Corey's tactics, he started to come back down the ladder, just as you set fire to the sage.

There was no flame, only thick, blue-gray smoke spiraling up from your hand, as if searching. With your breath you felt compelled to direct that search, blowing the smoke up toward Greegar to mingle with his stygian mantle. Like a mystery revealed, Greegar's cloak of mist began to recoil, sluggishly at first, then more quickly. It was like some cold-blooded reptile that at first doesn't know it has crawled onto a bed of hot coals, then can't get away fast enough, wiggling frantically into the thick of the inferno instead of out, in its pain and terror, then dashing free as the mist did now, sucked away by some invisible vortex in the night air.

What was left was only Greegar. Mean and nasty, and scary too, but only Greegar. The smoke blinded him for a moment and he rubbed his eyes as if waking up, dispossessed.

"Git that shit away from me." He tried to kick the smoldering sage out of your hand.

Corey quickly shoved the ladder away from the edge of the loft and Greegar tumbled to the barn floor at your feet. Corey began to look for something else to throw. Greegar scrambled up. You backed away, toward the gate leading into the corral. Greegar's face was twisted with rage. The horses circled wildly, snorting, breath steamy in the night air.

"Come here boy!" from Greegar.

You continue backing away.

"Run, Clint, run."

But you can't run. You would have to turn your back to him and that would mean taking your eyes off him, which you cannot do. The thought of his hands on you again is unbearable. You backed up against the gate. You can hear the horses right behind you. Greegar was only ten steps away. The horses have grown more and more nervous from the smell of the burning sage still glowing in your hand. Greegar moved closer, cautious now.

From Corey in the loft: "The horses, Clint, the horses. Let them out!"

You both moved at the same time. Greegar rushed forward as you groped behind for the wooden latch on the gate. You were slightly faster. You pulled the peg free, pushed the gate into the corral, and rushed in among the horses. They scattered before you, fearful of the smoky sage.

You moved across to the far side of the pen and then turned to drive them through the gate, past Greegar, and into the barn. They obliged at first but then Lady, the leader, stopped short as she sensed Greegar coming toward her. Without pausing, you threw the sage under her hooves and slapped her hard on the rump. She bolted through the gate, knocking Greegar aside. Buck, the two year old, and Star, Lady's colt, followed after, narrowly missing trampling Greegar.

Lady headed straight for underneath the loft, where usually she would try to scrape off her adolescent riders on the low-lying rafters. Corey, like Errol Flynn, swung over the side of the loft and onto her back. With a strong kick to her flanks and a yank on her mane he turned her back out, shouting, "Over here, Clinton, run!"

Greegar had scrambled to his feet and was coming straight for you. You dodged away from him as Corey dashed by on the horse.

Here is where the movie version of your escape ends.

Corey grabbed your outstretched arm and tried to pull you up onto the trotting horse, but he can't bring it off and hang onto the reinless horse at the same time. So he ended up half dragging you, half carrying you at the side of the running horse, out the other side of the barn, away from Greegar and onto the river road.

Once out of the barn, still dragging you, Corey directed the horse over to the fence that ran along the side of the road.

"Quick! Up on the fence. Hurry! Get on—no, in front. All right, let's go. You okay?"

"Yes. I think so."

"We can lose him if we get off the road. He won't be able to follow us in the truck."

Then a curse floated to us on the night air from the darkness of the barn.

"I ain't through with you yet. You're mine. Understand me? Fine. Don't sleep with your window open. In fact, don't sleep at all. Sleep is slaughtered for you. Murdered. You hear me? Dead!"

Some trick of the air made it seem as if he were right there just behind us whispering, hissing his malicious words in our ears, trying to frighten us.

Lady maintained her steady trot, off the road now and into the alfalfa field. You were nearly to the trees when the shock of what had almost happened hit you. What Greegar had tried to do to you. And something more.

"Did you see it? Did you Corey?"

"What?"

"Did you see what I saw?"

"I don't know."

"Don't know what you saw, or you didn't see it?"

Again, "I don't know."

"It was more than just Greegar. It was something from my nightmares. Something from the house." You began to tremble. It was not cold.

"Hey, it's okay. We got away, didn't we?"

"Ya, this time." Then, "It was his ghost."

"How could it be his ghost? He ain't dead yet."

"I don't know, but it was. Maybe not his own ghost, but his somehow. Somehow his."

A warm wind began to blow in your face as you sat on the front of the horse, but you could not stop trembling.

"It's okay, Clint. You're okay."

Awkwardness began to set in now. A lot had happened in the last half hour. What had drawn you downstairs? The moon? Why had you brought the sage? Why had its smoke had such affect on Greegar? Why did Greegar show up tonight just when he did? Whose voice was it that had told you to light the sage? And Corey naked. Greegar with his hands in your underpants. Corey naked next to you behind the cooler. What was it you were feeling? The burning sage. A sense of loathing mixed with desire flooded over you. The shame of it all began to burn your face.

"I think I'm going to be sick."

"Go ahead, man. I feel sick every time I see him."

Gorge rose in your throat, but you swallowed it back.

"You want me to stop Lady so you can get down for a minute?"

"No, don't stop. I'm okay now."

"You know, you're a tough little shit. I didn't know you had it in you. You're okay."

"What about you, Tarzan?" And something shifted. "You're not so bad yourself."

"Well . . . you're better!"

"No, you are. I'm okay, but you're the best." A pause, then, "Except I thought you were going to jerk my arm out of the socket when you tried to pull me up on Lady. But I still think you're the best." Another pause, then shyly, "And I'm next to the best." And you allowed yourself, just slightly, to sink back into the curve of his body.

Then in some gentle acknowledgment he rested his

chin on your shoulder. "All right then. I'll be the best and you're next to the best, definitely."

Maybe it was facing the villain together that allowed this tenderness to begin to emerge. Who knows? But suddenly it was there, a delicate flower peeking through snow, and with a flash Corey's former ambivalence toward you came clear. The tormenting at school. The silent stares across the dinner table. The unspoken words hanging in the air. He was resisting this very tenderness, because he didn't know how to express it. No one had ever shown him. But for now, for this night, all questions seemed to be answered. So Greegar had given you the key. By uniting the two of you against him, Greegar had shown Corey his place. Your sinking back 'to be next to the best' had opened a door, had given Corey a kind of permission, had shown him how 'to be.' In protecting you from Greegar, Corey had found a way. Your melting into his shelter told him it was right.

None of this was spoken. How could it be? You were only boys. Where would you find the words? But the stars were brighter now as you continued silently along the banks of the river.

Then Corey interrupted your thoughts. "You know, I may be the best and you're definitely next to the best, but I think I got a splinter in my butt when we were hiding behind the cooler."

You started to laugh.

"You think that's funny?" But you could tell he was grinning too. "A splinter can be a very painful thing. And in this case very personal."

All that had just happened vanished, and the gentle lurchings of Lady as you entered the riverbed lulled you into being just boys again, on a moonlit night, with a warm wind blowing in your faces. You rocked and swayed on Lady's back, Corey's breath in one ear and then the other as he directed her into the current. The water covered her ankles. Corey urged her carefully on and the water rose. You both gripped her hard with your knees and she whinnied. The water was rising still, until now it was lapping at the belly of the horse. You stared at the water. Your feet were immersed. You heard the rush and roar of the river from where it quickened on below. Lady struggled and her mane jerked in Corey's hands. You felt his arms tense and your eyes narrowed to slits, measuring the water ahead. It ceased rising and you were in it a long time. Then you were out of it, the wetness falling away as you came out on the opposite bank, the horse shedding water like some sea creature returning to land.

There was no concern about where you were going. Musing silently, it seemed random, strange events were seeking to control your lives. Strange things, even deadly, and somehow desire was wrapped up in all of it. You wouldn't think about it. You'd spend as much time alone as possible, in sunlight. You would draw, maybe draw Corey, and watch out for Greegar. Yes, with your books and your drawing, sunlight and Corey.

Corey broke the silence.

"Lady must be entranced by the moon."

"I guess so."

Lady was an old mare that didn't usually like to be ridden. Quite often, once you did get on her, she'd try to scrape you off by running under a low-hanging tree branch or shed roof. You could never get the saddle on by yourself, so you'd have to coax her over to a fence and climb up, then jump. Usually one of two things would happen: either she'd smash your knee up against the fence or move away just as you jumped, and you'd end up on your backside in the dirt. You'd also been stepped on, bit, and bucked off into ditches and thorn bushes. She seemed to mind Corey though.

"What did you do to get her to be so well-behaved?"

"I sneaked up on her one night when she was asleep and gave her a kiss. She's loved me ever since."

"Maybe she saw your dick and mistook you for the daddy of her kids."

"Very funny, wild man," and he knuckled your head.

After crossing the river, the trees cleared away a bit and moonlight pointed out wild roses growing through the remnants of a wooden fence. There had been a cabin there once. Hollyhocks marked a path, their dry stalks lining the way.

I remember that night as if it were etched permanently on the retina of my memory. How Corey's hands rested lightly on my thighs. How the horse led the way through the riverbed and the underbrush. But mostly what keeps coming back to me is the memory of the sound of his breath in my ears, one side and then the other, as he watched the way, letting Lady pick her path along slowly.

"Why do you think there is only one gravestone there on that hill?"

"What gravestone? Where?"

"Over there. In back of us a little now."

You watched him as he pointed and the profile of his face was of such transcendent beauty you winced as if struck and your breath fled your chest in a deep sigh.

"You okay?"

"Ya, sure. Next-to-the-best!"

"Maybe a homesteader that didn't make it through the winter," he answered himself. "The Vinegar Man would know."

"I've never been down this way before."

"I have. I've followed Greegar down here, lots of times. The bridge across to Rivertown is just through them trees. They get drunk and play cards. Maybe get in a fight. Mary stays down here, too."

"Crazy Mary?"

"She ain't so crazy. She helps the Vinegar Man make his wine. He shared a bottle with me once. He told me he was one of the first homesteaders in these parts some thirty years ago."

You moved through the trees and out into the open again. The breeze blew the smell of a skunk around, and you could hear bullfrogs close by.

"Your brother, John, joined the Army?"

Corey was silent.

"John joined up didn't he?"

"Ya." The frogs went silent in sympathy. "Ya, he did. And left me alone with that bastard. Let's go for a swim."

You had come upon Rivertown's fishing hole, a pond fed by flood waters and kept fresh by a natural spring. Corey slipped down and led the horse to a hitching tree. Voices floated over from Rivertown and their campfire was a firefly flickering through the willows.

"They'll be drinking all night. Just don't make too much noise in case Greegar has rejoined them. Sound carries. I'm sure that's where he'd been earlier tonight."

He turned to step out of his levis. You jumped sideways off the horse. You weren't sure you wanted to get wet. Corey tossed his pants aside and walked down the muddy bank and eased into the water without making a sound. Moonlight rippled. He submerged for a long breath and reappeared further out, silently swimming away, then back. You sat to hold down a rock at the edge of the water and folded your arms. It wasn't cold. Corey treaded water. Voices drifted over from Rivertown again

"It's warm. Come in." Corey swam back. "Last winter, while you was laid up, John and me came over here and the pond was froze over. That don't usually happen. It don't get cold enough for long enough. For some reason we decided to skate on the surface, but took off our clothes so they wouldn't get wet. Crazy, hunh? John left soon after that."

A fish jumped, or a frog. The moon moved behind a cloud. You decided to undress.

"There's something scary about water at night."

Instead of laughing Corey agreed. "Except when the water's warm. Then it ain't so bad."

Your skin was white in the moonlight. The water was warm. Voices drifted. You didn't speak. Corey swam out and back. You stood in the shallows chest deep, occasionally dunking under. The horse foraged in the weeds.

Corey climbed onto the bank and silently shook himself dry, tossing his mane of hair, like Hiawatha. You stood and dripped, then after a moment sat gingerly, on a tree stump. The warm breeze wrapped the two of you, beginning to towel you the rest of the way dry. Corey lay down in a grassy spot, still naked.

"You ever feel like getting a girl?"

Actually you had, but you hadn't. At least not the way Corey was thinking. Once you had a dream about a dark-haired woman whom you took to be your mother. You woke up feeling guilty and aroused. You looked between Corey's legs and away. He noticed.

"You ever jerk off?"

You had, but not lately. The idea of pleasure being connected to your dick, since the operation, had been put aside. You felt nervous and excited.

"I bet I can get off faster than you." He took hold of himself.

Once, when still in the hospital, with the tube in it, you had decided to try and get hard, to see. But it hurt and you immediately stopped. You watched Corey concentrating on himself, then realized you'd gotten stiff. Corey leaned back. You remembered pouring water over him in the cornfield during last year's harvesting. You touched yours. Corey's had started to get stiff and tall. Maybe because yours was shorter you got hard faster. You smiled at Corey. He didn't see. He continued to lengthen. Lady stopped foraging and raised her head.

Corey whispered, "How's it going?"

You paused, distracted. His was fully extended now.

"You want to touch it?" You shook your head and he said, "That's okay. Look." He showed you as cream poured out of his dick and spilled over his hand. You looked surprised. He groaned a bit and shuddered.

"What's the matter? You don't have cum yet?"

You shook your head and the breeze brought you the smell of him.

He laughed. "That's okay. Don't worry, you will."

You felt relieved. He wiped his hand on the grass.

"John taught me how to jack-off. Mine is bigger than his, even bigger than Greegar's. So John said anyway. He should know."

CHAPTER THREE

THAT YEAR, as you grew stronger, began a series of circuitous journeys for you and Corey. You would go reeling out to work the fields in the morning, or meandering down to the river or into the hills, fledglings rushing out and away to come spiraling back at dusk. You explored the rapids below the dam and under the railroad bridge. Each new place was a conquest. Many Saturdays were spent raiding the pigeon nests beneath the bridge, or stalking deer, or spearing carp and suckers in the shallows below the rapids where the river broadened out and ran through the Wagstaff's place, next on.

Corey discovered he could hang off the side of the railroad bridge with one arm and pull pigeon squabs out of their nests, while suspended over the water, mythic in his fearlessness. Somewhere along one of these journeys you were promoted from tag-along to co-conspirator and he would hand the young birds up to you before swinging onto the next support beam.

Weaving paths out and away from the farm house, you cast yourselves each day into the morning light, down the hill, through the fields, then upriver or down. Sometimes you wandered so far, lacing footprints in the dust or sand or leaves, just the two of you, that the evening sun, splashing through the clouds, would find you rushing back the way you'd come to find familiar ground before dark.

Slowly, it seemed that you were coming to trust one another. So it came to pass that wherever Corey would go, you would go. Whatever he would end up doing you would be a part of it. You laid down in front of him the right to be leader, and easily, as children do, you laid down yourself as well. You calculated no gain in giving this gift, in your willingness to follow him, and didn't try to figure out your reasons for doing so. That these things came to be that season seemed as inevitable as the weather, the changing of the leaves, the waxing and waning of the moon. Once he began to accept your wanting him for a friend, all questions seemed to be resolved.

Quite often you would come across the Vinegar Man or Greegar on these outings. Automatically you would avoid being seen by Greegar, or, if you thought you could get away with it and there was nothing else to do, you would spy on him during his drinking bouts at Rivertown. Always in the back of your head was the night of the full moon, when he seemed to be anointed by the Ghost from your nightmares and the memory of his icy hand inside your shorts.

On the other hand, when you came across the Vinegar Man and Mary, you would join them. Sometimes it would be fishing or gathering herbs. Sometimes it would be picking wild asparagus or currants to be used in making wine. If his memories weren't troubling him or he hadn't had too much to drink, the Vinegar Man was a wealth of stories of the old days and would direct you to places off the beaten path; to old Indian campgrounds or the remains of an abandoned homestead or a fishing hole you hadn't yet discovered for yourselves.

One Saturday, when you'd brought along camping gear and your inevitable sketchbook, you found him and Mary picking cherries near the Rivertown fishing hole not far from the headstone you'd stumbled across the night of your escape from Greegar. The Vinegar Man was having one of his bad days. So when he spoke there was a dark edge to his voice and little indication of the powerful Shaman who had given you the sage that had helped protect you from Greegar.

"Where you boys off to this time?"

"Oh, just out and away. How are the cherries?"

"Good, this year. Good. Found some currants yesterday."

Mary smiled, tilted her head sideways and added, "Black ones. They're the sweetest."

You shook off your packs and set down your fishing poles and joined in gathering the fruit.

"One for the bucket. One for me. Two for the bucket. Three for me." Mary paused from filling her skirt to weave columbine in her hair.

"Mary, Mary, quite contrary, eats more than she picks." The Vinegar Man paused, reflecting. "Polly Bemis planted these trees here some forty years ago. Every time I come here I think of her and Charlie. That wasn't her real name. What was it? Oh, yes. Lalu. Lalu Nathoy. That was it. She was a Chinese girl, fourteen years old when she first

73

came to these parts, barely four feet tall. She outlived Charlie some twenty years. They had a homestead right there." He nodded northward. "Right there through the trees. That's Charlie's marker. Polly is buried over in Grangeville. It's a shame. She should be here, near her cherry trees and the river."

Part of the walls of the old homestead and the chimney could be seen through the willows from where you stood.

The Vinegar Man continued, but his voice trembled now. "It all burned down one day. Chicken pens empty, the cabin door swinging open. She's gone, with Melissa now."

His voice trailed away and you whispered to Corey, "Who is Melissa?"

"I don't know."

It was clear the Vinegar Man had fallen into a day-dream then, whispering to himself, lost in another time, another place. Mary moved over to him and placed a hand on his grizzled brow. It was as if he saw someone there, some dark and troublesome swan that had surfaced from the murky bottom of the pond, and he called her name. "Melissa!" Then again, "Melissa." He rambled on, forgetting we were there.

"Melissa like the mountains. Melissa and the homestead. Even before the first cold, we knew we wouldn't have enough to last through the winter. She wouldn't let me give up. She sent me into the town. Into Grangeville.

"'One more packing trip. Before the freeze sets in,' she said. 'Then we'll be all right. Then we'll make it.' She'd be okay alone. She'd be all right. 'Go,' she said, 'go.' Melissa in the mountains, and me in town, working hard, dreaming of that beautiful woman. I left her. I left her alone."

"Shush now, Viktor. It's over and done." This from Mary still caressing his brow.

Then, in his delirium: "I didn't want to go. I didn't want to leave you, Melissa.

"Hush little baby don't say a word, Mama's going to buy you a Mockingbird. And if that Mockingbird don't sing, Mama's going to buy you a diamond ring.

"She'd be all right, she said, her and the baby. Goddamn her and goddamn the Vinegar Man drinking to forget. If only I could forget what I found when I got back to the homestead. What I found written in blood on the sheets."

Something broke in his face then and he turned to Mary, stricken. "I'm sorry, Melissa. I'm sorry. Hush little baby don't say a word, Mama's going to buy you a Mockingbird . . . "

His eyes clouded over then, and he drifted into an unintelligible conversation with himself, in which his hands performed a twitching accompaniment of gestures.

After a moment he came back.

"Melissa gave Polly and Charlie the seeds for these trees on the day they got married. She had brought them all the way from back East. Mary and I still pick them for her. These trees will outlast us all."

Corey said, "It's good we have the cherries still, isn't it?" He dumped big handfuls of ripe fruit in Mary's basket.

"Yes, it is good," and then slowly the old man's sparkle came back. "The last time I saw Polly she was a little old woman. Still neat as a pin and not much over four feet tall. She was wrinkled as a walnut and full of dash and charm. She still rolled from side to side when she walked.

The strangest kind of gait. I guess they bound her feet up when she was a little girl, the way they did girl babies those days in China. It didn't seem to slow her down much. She ran up and down the hills like a squirrel looking for nuts in a pine tree. I remember asking her, 'Where's Charlie?'

"She told me, 'Abed. He been abed most two years now. He pretty closs too. I gotta pack grub all time. Alla time!'

"Charlie better watch out or he's going to lose you to some handsome cowboy!

"'Hee! Hee! Yes I think so too.'

"I was running a pack train to the mining camps in those days. It was the spring of 1882 when I first saw Polly and . . . Melissa. That was the same year Charlie Bemis got shot over some fool card game."

As the Vinegar Man began to reminisce, you took your sketchpad out of your backpack and began to draw. Corey made himself comfortable on a rock near Mary, and the Vinegar Man's tale unfolded.

The Vinegar Man, known as Viktor then, had taken a homestead north of Warren in the Salmon River mountains. From his ranch he would pack in supplies to the hungry miners several times a year. He'd come into "E-dah-hoe" over the century-old Lolo Trail, the route the Indians took into the buffalo country of Montana. He'd been hunting buffalo himself when he wandered into the new territory and ended up staying.

The Lolo was the same taken by Lewis and Clark

eighty years before. First the trappers came into the new land, and then the miners when gold was first discovered by E.D. Pierce in 1860. The miners were followed by the packers and traders, not long after by the settlers.

Viktor ran his pack train from Thunder Mountain, *Tome-up-yaggi* (the place where the clouds cry), to Warren to Florence, sometimes continuing on north to Grangeville, where he would lay in for supplies. His trains would average between fourteen to twenty animals. Each carried an average of three hundred pounds. This weight had to be distributed evenly to balance the load or on the steep mountain trails disaster was inevitable. Lashing and tying was an art. Especially when Viktor was doing the tying using diamond and squaw hitches.

Bears were not uncommon and their presence would cause a lot of trouble. Pack mules and horses would buck and bolt at the very scent of one. Viktor had, on more than one occasion, lost his supplies or had them ruined because of bears.

The heaviest load would be placed on the lead animal to set the pace. Viktor would travel steadily for six to eight hours and average twelve to fifteen miles a day, depending on the weather or if the trail was climbing, descending, or crossing flats.

Viktor knew where the grass was greenest, where water was handiest, and which places along the way made the best campgrounds. Upon leaving his homestead, Viktor would lead his pack train fifteen miles along the south fork of the Salmon River, then up a steep mountainside, where he would join up with a well-traveled Indian trail. Then his journey into Warren was through open pines and grass, and he would ford the south fork to enter a forest of fir and dwarfed tamarack, then on through beds of lava and manzanita, finally to reach the summit and snow, where he joined the Warren wagon trail.

When he would stop, the animals would have to be unloaded and the pack saddles lined up against a log or boulder for the night. The lead animal would be tied up wearing a bell. The animals would have to be watched constantly to prevent them from straying too far. Usually they would stay nearby, but Viktor would take no chances.

It took considerable time to re-pack and cinch, so Viktor's day would begin at dawn and he would employ one or two helpers depending upon the size, weight, and number of the loads. His most regular assistant was an old Nez Percé medicine man named Many Wounds, who seemed to appear out of nowhere whenever Viktor was putting together a train.

The traffic into Warren would vary depending upon where rumor was leading the California miners who came pouring into the area. Some headed for Elk City, some for *See-nimp*, Buffalo Hump, or Florence, or Mount Idaho.

Once on the wagon trail the descent into Warren was through a wide flat basin choked with a dense growth of spruce, here and there opening up into a beautiful little meadow filled with marsh grass and wildflowers. And then came the mines.

Viktor stayed on the packing side of the mining business, not being particularly fond of the jostling mass of frenzied humanity he would find each time he entered the mining camp. Even during the Thunder Mountain excitement in the early 1900s he left the digging to the green-horns who flocked in by the hundreds.

These numbers were swelled by the thousands of

Celestials (as the Chinese miners were called), who were released from work on the railroad when the Central Pacific and the Union Pacific joined up at Promontory Point. For the next forty years the Celestials swarmed through the camps to grind out a living from claims with pickings too lean to interest the fevered white men.

So Viktor kept himself separate from all this madness; the gambling, the whoring, and the opium (known as Chinese Candy) that the Celestials brought with them. He never talked much, but he knew a lot. He read voraciously when the homestead was covered under snow, too deep and too fresh to allow the pack animals to get out. Hour after hour he would read on long winter days. His philosophy was simple, marked by solitude, but enriched by the culture he found in books and the wildlife he found in the mountains surrounding him.

Of all the frontiersmen to be found on the periphery of the mining communities of central Idaho, Viktor grew to be the most adept. Seldom did he need to search for game. He always seemed to know where to find it. He was a creature of the forest. The meadows and valleys were his front step, the mountains his rooftop. When he walked into a room it was as if he were still out of doors.

It was on a packing trip into Warren that Viktor first saw Melissa and he said to himself, "Now there's a beautiful woman." And he understood more than ever why there was a need for Mozart and Shakespeare, a need for something to explain what ordinary words couldn't.

Viktor had stopped into Charlie Bemis's saloon for a beer. He had just finished a tough haul into Warren and was looking forward to getting back to his homestead and letting his animals rest up. That was his intention at least, until he saw Melissa working behind the bar at Charlie's. He ended up staying in Warren an extra three days. For a man rarely seen in the same spot two days running it was unusual behavior, or it would have been if anyone had noticed. But Viktor had the same ability a wild animal has of willing himself invisible. So for three days he did just that. He faded into the background and watched Melissa work.

Melissa was not perfect of face or figure. But her bones balanced together in so gracious a fashion, so profoundly, that as he watched her walk and stand and lean, he understood things he'd never even thought about before. His world began to have an additional charm and his life a new kind of balance from the first moment of seeing her.

Melissa was an independent woman. The daughter of a newspaperman in St. Louis, she had been schooled in all the arts, particularly opera. In spite of the protests of her domineering father, who wanted her to confine her singing to the concert stage, Melissa began to entertain on the showboats up and down the Mississippi River. It was there she began to be entranced by the tales she heard of the wild west, and she began to despise the high-society life of her father and St. Louis. So when the opportunity came, she joined a wagon train heading for the Oregon Trail. Hearing of the gold rush in Idaho, a group had broken off from the original party and Melissa had gone with them to end up in Warren.

The biggest saloon in town was owned by Charlie Bemis. Basically a lazy man, Charlie had retired from prospecting and invested his money in a saloon-hotel that had a barbershop and a bathhouse attached. For two bits a miner could get a bath and a shave. For a dollar more, clean sheets and a place to spend the night. Charlie had worked out a deal with the Chinese laundry across the street.

One of the few single women in Warren, it was easy for Melissa to become Charlie's right hand, running the bar most days and occasionally entertaining the miners, cardsharks, and frontiersmen who would frequent the place.

She'd been approached by them all: cattlemen, trappers, and prospectors—men hungry for female companionship. Some were lean, some husky, some generous, and some mean, but Melissa was waiting. She wasn't sure what it was she was waiting for, but she knew it hadn't happened yet. So she worked and sang and took delight in this new-found land that had come to be her home.

Melissa didn't notice Viktor at all those first three days, even though he sat in the same place each day with a book. It was a slow afternoon that first time he saw her. She was in a melancholy mood and so she began to sing a sweet song of unrequited love. Before long Charlie joined in on his fiddle and the walls of the barroom began to dissolve, and Melissa and those listening were transported into the world of her dreams.

She began quietly, to herself, while she tidied up and then incidentally she turned around and the full force of her beauty struck Viktor like a hammer blow. She did not notice, enrapt in her song, but Viktor found himself suddenly having difficulty breathing and the beer glass he'd just lifted nearly slipped from his fingers.

So Viktor—this tall, gruff, silent man—found himself hurrying to get his livestock home and rushing back to Warren, hoping for another glimpse of what he'd seen that first afternoon. Overnight he turned into a poet.

He found himself praying: "Let her beauty teach my frowns a more beguiling look. Let me love and be loved."

Until now he had been forged and formed by his solitary life in the wilderness, and though he was not humorless, his countenance could be mistaken for foreboding, in the way a mountain is foreboding. Certainly his social skills were almost non-existent. He could woo a marmot into his stew pot or seduce a trout onto a hook, but a woman? For the first time in his life the strength of his arm and the length of his stride were not enough, mere trifles.

So, for a month and a day, Viktor came to hear Melissa sing. He never said a word, averting his gaze and pretending to read his book whenever she glanced in his direction. He watched her and composed poetry in his imagination.

She never really noticed him as different, just another frontiersman holding up the end of the bar day after day. Quieter than most. Better looking than most. Nothing special, except maybe the way his big hand closed all the way around a beer glass, and the way he would lean into her without looking at her when she would sing certain songs in the afternoon.

About this time, Cherokee Bob and English Dan came into town. They brought with them a breath of bad air. Usually whiskey-drunk, Cherokee Bob was a half-breed and a horse thief. English Dan wore a bowler and sported a fancy six-shooter. The two of them arriving in town at the same time was a bad sign.

They came, rowdy, into Charlie's, galloping through town on the way in. The Bad Guys: Cherokee Bob and English Dan. To survive, they took, not from the land, like the miners, but from men. And like the miners, they took without asking.

Dan strode in first, boldly. Cherokee Bob, more of a weasel, slunk in sideways, willing himself invisible. Smallpox scars had ruined his face and so he hated being looked at. He had big meaty arms and a foul temper.

Dan headed straight for the bar. "Hey Charlie, bring your tired ass over here. I need a drink."

Viktor glanced over at the two of them.

"What are you looking at?" snarled Cherokee Bob.

Viktor said nothing.

"Charlie! Whiskey!"

Charlie Bemis placed a shot glass and a bottle down in front of English Dan.

"Hey, what about me." This from Cherokee Bob. "I'll take some of that, if it's going cheap. What's the matter? You only got one clean glass? Or maybe you don't like half-breeds. Maybe you don't like my pretty face?"

Charlie took his time wiping off another glass and then slid it down the bar to the waiting Indian.

"I hear they's takin' out twenty-five dollars a day at Thunder Mountain." Dan tossed back a drink. "What do you hear, Packer? Hey, Melissa give us a song." Then, without waiting for an answer, "Charlie, bring a bottle. Let's have some poker."

Charlie looked over, but made no move.

"What've you got to lose, boys? Let's see some stakes."

"These stakes enough?" A greenhorn with a bag of gold dust burning a hole in his pocket moved up to the bar.

Dan measured the pouch and the greenhorn. "Good enough for starters, I'd say. Let's have at it." They moved over toward an empty table. "Come on, Melissa, let's hear somethin' good. Charlie, you want us to deal you in or not?"

Charlie took another bottle off the shelf. "Take a table and keep your feet off the chairs. We want the shit to stay on the floor."

"Ya, ya. Deal the cards."

Dan straddled a chair, feet tapping a beat, hands never still.

"Deal 'em up. Bring a glass for Mr. Bemis, Melissa. We know how Charlie likes to drink and play poker. Let's go. This boy," referring to the greenhorn, "has money I want to take." Twitching and jumping, he tossed off another drink.

They settled in. The game stayed even. The piano man began to pick out a syncopated melody. Cherokee Bob stared at his cards stoically. Then there was a shift, and English Dan began to lose. First to Charlie, then two hands in a row to the greenhorn. When he lost a fourth time, again to the greenhorn, Dan jerked his chair around, stood up, and walked to the bar.

Sawdust covered the wood floor. A big fireplace stood opposite the swinging door. The upright piano was at the end of the long bar, surrounded by ten or twelve tables and chairs.

"Hey, Melissa. What about that song? I need a change of luck."

"It's pretty hard to sing and tend to the bar at the same time."

"You're a many-talented woman, I hear. All the way from Saint Louie. I can see they're raising 'em healthy back East just from looking at you. So now I want to know if it sounds as good as it looks. I like a woman that moans a little. If you know what I mean." And he slapped down a five-dollar gold piece onto the bar.

"Yes, I do know what you mean, Mister Dan English, or whatever your name is. And I would think that any woman that got anywhere near you would have to start moaning just to be able to stand it. You know what I mean?"

"No need to get nasty, sister. I paid my money. Now I want a song, goddamn it!"

"I'm not your sister. And I sing for who I want, when I want. Is that clear? Besides, the way you been playing, it looks like you'd better keep your money for the next hand."

"Why you slimy, little stuck-up bitch!" And he started to move toward her. But suddenly he found himself face to face with Viktor's six-foot six-inches of towering rage.

"I don't know where you got so swelled up in yourself. But don't mess with this woman. She's way out of your league." And Viktor placed a heavy hand on English Dan's raised arm.

Dan twisted away and made a move for his gun. Melissa moved closer to Viktor.

"Careful, Dan." Charlie had taken out his gun and placed it on the table. "Many self-important pups like yourself have found themselves dropping in the dust before their guns left leather when they tried to call out Viktor long-legs here. And besides, I don't believe I like you messin' with the best back-up a saloon keeper ever had."

English Dan hesitated, looking slowly from Viktor to Charlie and back again. It was a well-known fact that Charlie could keep a beer can rolling with a six-shooter. So with a sneer, Dan turned back to Melissa. "Missy, you are one lucky little girl. If we was alone you'd be on your knees where I'd have a few things to show you about a woman's place."

"You don't have nothing to show me I haven't already seen before. And the day I get on my knees to you will be the day pigs fly."

"Pigs and blue jays would be moving in together if we was alone, missy."

Viktor's rage had turned him to granite and he placed himself between the foul-mouthed outlaw and Melissa.

Charlie caressed his gun fondly, "You need to get some air, English." Then, as he could see Dan was going to back down, "When you've got your licker under control, maybe we can finish this game we started.—unless this little diversion is your way of getting out of a losing game?"

"Deal the cards. I ain't through with any of you yet."

Melissa cleaned the bar near Viktor.

"Harsh words, son. You need to learn to smile when you're losing. It hurts less." Charlie began to shuffle the cards again, but he left his gun where it lay on the table.

And now Melissa and Viktor spoke together for the first time.

"Thank you for stepping in. Not necessary, but appreciated."

Viktor settled onto a stool at the bar. His face softened and, as if versing love, he simply said, "My pleasure." Inside he felt as if the seasons altered and certain stars left their course. Made bold by her nearness, he continued: "I've never known or felt anything that could move me like a sunset or the rain, until I heard you sing." He dropped his eyes.

She watched his face as he stared into his glass, watched it melt and reform. He looked up then and the full force of her beauty struck him again. "I've always been alone. Let your beauty teach me companionship the way it has taught me desire."

At his words, she sighed and half-whispered to herself, "Ah, he is the one who knows." They fell silent then, suddenly not knowing what to say or how to move.

Just then, Chan Lee from the laundry across the street entered the saloon. An obsequious Celestial, he was always burning punk sticks in his shop to ward off evil. Most days he could be seen walking calmly from the laundry to his garden plot on the outskirts of town with his hands clasped behind his back, his pigtail swaying in time. But now something was up. He was out of breath and his usually inscrutable face exuded excitement.

When he spoke it was to Charlie. But first he bowed three times, out of politeness, and then covered his mouth, as if afraid the words might spill out too quickly. "Mister Charlie Bemis, sir. So very sorry, Charlie, to be disturbing your poker game. I just receive important information." Then he waited, nearly bursting, for permission to continue.

"Well, what is it, Chan Lee?"

"Big shipment, Charlie, just come in over in Grangeville. My friend, Chinaman Sam. Supplies and—" he looked around the room to be sure he had everyone's attention "—girls! All the way from Hong Kong! He need help coming over mountains."

The last part went unheard because of the whooping and hollering set up by Cherokee Bob, Dan, and the other men scattered around the saloon. Girls from Hong Kong meant only one thing. The Chinese never brought their wives over and they never married white women, preferring to send their earnings and their dead home to China. So the girls would be free and easy and available. Well, maybe not free, but probably available.

"Girls from Hong Kong! How many, Chan Lee?"

"I no know for sure. Three maybe four."

"Yahoo! I got first dibs. Chinee girls are the best." This from Cherokee Bob.

"How would you know? You ain't never had nothin' but squaw meat."

"Well, that's about to change, ain't it?" Then a light went off in Cherokee Bob's head and he pulled English Dan aside and spoke in lowered tones that went unnoticed in all the commotion.

"Hey, wait a minute, English." Cherokee Bob spoke from the side of his mouth. "Supplies from Hong Kong will mean Chinese Candy and it sounds like, from the way Chan Lee is acting, that there could be lots of it. We need to get outside and have a little conversation."

"Hey, Charlie, how about we finish this? And just to show no hard feelings, let me buy the bar a drink."

English Dan put down money and hurried outside with Cherokee Bob at his side.

Chan Lee continued, "Many supplies come with girls. My friend, Chinaman Sam, send word he need packer with big gun and strong horses."

"Hey, Viktor. This sounds like a job for you."

Viktor nodded, still under the spell he and Melissa had cast upon themselves.

"You're a packer?"

"Yes, a packer. I work out of my homestead, north of here."

"You'll be going to Grangeville then?"

"Yes, to Grangeville."

Then in some further, gentle acknowledgment of what was passing between them, he took her hand and said, "The Shoshonis have a legend of a bright object falling from the skies and resting upon a mountain, forever shining, and some say, forever inaccessible. They call it *e-dah-hoe*. Once seen, they say it is never forgotten. They say that if a man is lucky enough to see it, he must always come circling back." His hand completely covered both of hers and she knew he meant her.

"I can hope you'll be back then?" And it was her turn to drop her eyes.

"Count on it." Then from the book in front of him, he quoted, "If you'll but promise to teach me how you look and with what art you sway the motion of my heart."

Unable to speak, Melissa watched him stand and turn to walk out the door.

As he disappeared she heard him say, "I pray your beauty will teach my frowns a more beguiling look."

And she repeated to herself again, "My beauty, his frowns? He is the one who knows. The one I've been waiting for."

CHAPTER FOUR

THE NEWS that Chinese girls were on their way spread around Warren like a brush fire. Miners rushed to book up the few rooms in the hotel. Men who hadn't shaved or bathed for the whole summer (unless they fell into the creek) started showing up at Charlie's beardless and clean. Melissa and Charlie were busy keeping all the extra bellies full of beer and grub. Between onslaughts, they did what they could to tidy up the place and stock the kitchen and answer questions. The whole town took on a festive air, even though it would be at least ten days before Viktor was back with the new arrivals. Charlie would be making a big profit.

It was the first time Viktor was sorry to leave behind the chaos of the mining town. He made his preparations for departure quickly, in a dream, the sense of Melissa clinging to him like ivy to an oak. Even so, he did not look back as he sent his big chestnut horse up the gentle, grassy slope out of town. He reasoned that the sooner he was off the sooner he would be back. His homestead lay seven miles north of Warren, near where the south fork joined the Salmon River. Midmorning he stopped at the homestead to collect his pack animals and the rest of the supplies he would need. It was his only stop that day. He crossed the Salmon soon after, and entered the forest trail that would lead him to the Clearwater and the second leg of his trip. He hardly noticed.

His saddlebags were light. If all went well, he would be in Grangeville in three days. It would be the return trip that would be slow. The animals would be loaded down and the place would be set to accommodate the women.

Late afternoon the first day, a bank of ominous clouds showing dark at the base began to build in the sky above the mountains. A thunderstorm would hit before sundown. Viktor watched the building clouds anxiously. A lot of rain would make the river-crossing dangerous on the return trip.

He was half-way to Elk City when the rain began. He continued without pause. The rain and the extra animals only slowed him a little. He had covered nearly twenty-five miles by sunset. It was a record time. The rain had been light and disappeared entirely as he came upon a small clearing in the towering forest and decided to stop for the day. To the west, the sun was rapidly sinking into the hills. To the east, the light stole down the mountain peaks. He tethered his animals and laid out his bedroll before building a fire.

Viktor's mind whirled with emotion. Many times, as he went about his work that night, he stopped, entranced by some image of Melissa he'd carried away with him from Warren. He stood at the edge of his campfire light and watched the stars come out and imagined what it would be like to have her there standing beside him. The next morning, watching the sun come up, he wondered the same. The world had never seemed so beautiful.

Early that day, just before Elk City, he joined up with the Clearwater, bypassing town. Midday a forlorn-looking family of Long Hairs, non-Christian Nez Percé, appeared through a tangle of fallen trees that blocked the trail. The oldest, Many Wounds, was a *Smokeller* or Dreamer of the Nez Percé tribe who often helped Viktor with his pack-trains. The Indian raised his hand to greet Viktor, who was known to most of the Long-Hairs in the area and respected.

There was nothing in their food pouches but wishes, so Viktor stopped and shared his food. There were four of them: two children, a woman, and the wizened old man. A few starved ponies made up the rest.

Viktor knew their ways, so he knew that Many Wounds, the elder, was a *te-wat*, or medicine man. The Dreamers were descendants of Smoholla, the great prophet who had foreseen the coming of the white man. Dispossessed of their tribal lands and decimated by sickness and disease, the Nez Percé had become a broken and scattered people, as their prophet had predicted. Some, who accepted the white man's ways and became Christian, survived, but lost their hearts. The majority had been driven onto a reservation. A few, such as these, who held to the Dreamer religion, disappeared into the wilderness and were seldom seen by white men.

Some said that the Dreamers began to sleep and wake no more the day Peli-Yevi was moved. Spaulding, a Methodist minister, was responsible for the desecration.

Peli-Yevi was an old man with very strong medicine, maybe too strong. He got in an argument with the creator, Hunyahwat, who turned Peli-Yevi into a pillar of stone. All the Indians knew the story of the granite pillar and had great respect for Hunyahwat's decision to turn Peli-Yevi into stone. They watched in horror when Spaulding moved the pillar from the place where it had resided for thousands of years and stood it in front of the mission church. It now bore a plaque honoring the Methodist ministry. Spaulding had moved a pillar of the gods and come to no harm.

From that day forward the Dreamers began to question the power of their dreams.

With dignity, the Nez Percé thanked Viktor for the food and he pushed on. When he turned to look back, they had all vanished, except for the *te-wat*. As if giving a gift, the Dreamer slowly pointed to a meadowlark circling overhead, and then disappeared into the forest. The song of the lark followed Viktor the rest of the day, even during the intermittent rain. Many Wounds most likely would find a safe campsite for the woman and the two children and join Viktor later in his journey.

Viktor sat up late staring into the campfire that night. Tomorrow would bring the final ascent into Grangeville and the beginning of his return to Melissa. The embers glowed, burning low. A chorus of crickets answered a solo. He mused aloud. "I pray her beauty will teach my frowns a more beguiling look." The night sounds gave accompaniment to his musing. "That I may know by what art she sways the motion of my heart."

In his passion, then, he stood and bowed low as if she were there. "Let your beauty teach me companionship the way it has taught me desire. Not taken for the expected nor the granted, but gifted by chance, thus the more treasured." In his delirium she took his hand and he danced. Like an elk, he danced. In some majestic animal-frenzy he bounded to his feet and tore the air with his arms. He froze. He took a breath and cried out joyously. "I pray our love will be ever a mystery, this quick bright thing, ever a mystery!" The sound echoed through the treetops in the still night. He stomped the ground. He ripped the air. He was a creature of the forest claiming his own. Then, like an eagle, he swooped low over the dying embers of his fire and hurled himself into the darkness to stop short, frozen, face to face with the old *te-wat*. Viktor took another breath and tried to still his racing heart. Many Wounds always seemed to get great pleasure out of taking Viktor by surprise. This time was no exception.

The Dreamer spoke in his native tongue. "You drive away demons very well."

Most Viktor understood, and so he smiled his thanks, somewhat abashed. Not because he'd been caught dancing in the dark, but because once again the Nez Percé had been able to come so close without him being aware.

The *te-wat* continued: "It is honor to witness." Then, with trembling accuracy, the old man began to dance Viktor's dance back to him. Viktor watched with astonishment. What had been a simple, joyous impulse, largely improvised, was transformed into a magical ritual when executed by the *te-wat*. The medicine man did him great honor. When Many Wounds had finished the dance he was silent for a moment and then said, "She will be safe now. At least for a time. Your dance has strong medicine."

They sat then and Many Wounds filled a pipe with a

mild preparation of aromatic leaves and bark with a light sprinkle of tobacco. The old Dreamer sat smoking in silence for a few minutes, then he returned the pipe to its pouch. Viktor listened quietly as the old man continued. He didn't understand all the words, but he knew.

"You dance the dance of one who wins. The victor. I know no such dances now."

Viktor stirred the fire. The *te-wat*'s gaze pierced him through the darkness.

"We dance on bended knees. Come down from Hunyahwat, who gave us the Mother Earth." The medicine man made four stately gestures to the four corners and a rasping chant began to emanate from deep within him. Then, in a piteous supplication, a lamentation to that unseen incomprehensible power that had allowed the land to be to taken from his people, the aged *te-wat* fell to his knees and dragged himself through the campfire. Viktor, knowing, made no move to go to him. The *te-wat* slowly got to his feet. He was not burned.

"I will dance no more, for always. It is fitting that a good white man, one who dances, one who knows, should see my last dance. You must remember, my friend." He rambled on. "The earth is the Mother of all life. She has turned her face away. For many moons I have traveled without her protection. To see her again I must return to her bosom. I long for her. My time is nearly finished. The souls of the blameless are carried on the backs of birds to paradise."

The *te-wat* gazed deeply into the fire still as a stone. Finally, he spoke again. It was directly to Viktor in the voice of a dreamer that he spoke. "She who brings the greatest joy, brings great grief as well."

The two men, woodsman and *te-wat*, sang to each other that night. One of lost love, one of newfound. And it was the most tender thing.

Viktor fell asleep to the sound of the *te-wat*'s voice.

"The white man said to me, 'Work!' I shall never work. Men who work cannot dream, and wisdom comes to us in dreams. They ask me to plough the ground. Shall I take a knife and tear my Mother's bosom? They ask me to dig for stone. Shall I dig under her skin for her bones? They ask me to cut the grass and make hay and sell it and be rich. But dare I cut off my Mother's hair? The white man has taken my Mother, my wife, myself, from me. I will dance no more, for always."

The last thing Viktor seemed to hear before falling into a deep sleep was the *te-wat* speaking his name. "You must dream for the land now, Viktor. You are the one who wins. I am finished. It is done." And while Viktor slept he dreamed he was a sentinel guarding the earth. And the earth was Melissa.

Viktor woke before sunrise. As always, Many Wounds had slipped away, before morning light, leaving no sign. It was as if he had never been there, except for Viktor's lingering dream.

It took the morning to climb out of the Clearwater River valley. Just before the summit Many Wounds rejoined Viktor. The *te-wat* didn't consider following Viktor's packtrain work. It was understood that he would come and go as he wished. In reality much of Viktor's initial success as a packer had come about because Many Wounds had taken him under his wing. Like the night before, the medicine man had come to teach Viktor much more than packing.

The view at the top was of rolling hills to the south and a prairie spreading to the horizon in the west. In the recent past the prairie had been filled with camas bulbs, a main staple for the Nez Percé, who would harvest the roots and bake them in the earth. To be good, camas had to remain in the hot earth overnight. Now the once-infinite prairie was filling up with farms and the camas was gone.

Mount Idaho, another mining camp, lay just north of the summit. Grangeville, the center of commerce for the mining district, was a few miles further on. Word of the packer's arrival preceded Viktor into Grangeville. Chinaman Sam was waiting at the stable on the outskirts of town. He seemed nervous, anxious to be on his way. His disquiet seemed amplified by the presence of Many Wounds.

While Viktor bedded down his livestock they discussed terms. Sam reluctantly agreed it would be better to begin the return to Warren in the morning, when the animals were fed and rested. Victor turned back to his animals as he said, "Tomorrow at first light I'll be in front of the hotel." Sam bowed and took his leave.

Viktor was paid as much as twenty-five cents a pound to pack in supplies, usually five to fifteen cents per pound. He earned his money. He packed everything from news to foodstuffs, tools, and large machinery parts. He was the lifeline to the outside world.

The first trip Many Wounds and Viktor had ever made together they packed a fly wheel for a Corliss steam engine into Warren. It was to be installed in a mill. It was ten feet in diameter with a ten-inch rim. It was packed in two sections slung between six mules. A storm came up and lightning struck the wheel and killed the six mules carrying it. Six more mules were hurried to the scene and the wheel was removed from the dead animals and re-slung. When Many Wounds learned the fly wheel was to be used in cutting up trees in a sawmill, he refused to help any further and disappeared, leaving the white men to finish the trip alone.

Viktor spent the afternoon in Grangeville gathering supplies for the miners in Warren—flour and beans and salt and other staples. He figured leaving four of the mules free for the baggage of Sam and the Chinese girls. The Celestials had their own horses for riding.

By daybreak Viktor and the *te-wat* had the animals organized and were waiting outside the hotel when Sam appeared with the first load of baggage. Quickly and efficiently Viktor strapped the baggage to the pack mules and was waiting when Sam returned with a second load and the girls. There were three of them. The two older ones had painted faces and were wearing western clothes. They obviously knew where they were going and what they were in for.

The third, however, was a girl in peasant clothes, not more than a child. She appeared to be lame. She was tiny and had a pretty face. Maybe because of her strange side-to-side walk, and because she was so small, she gave the impression of being a wind-up doll on the brink of losing her balance. She rushed about waiting on the older girls. They ignored her. So did Sam.

"Hey, little thing, let me help you with that." The tiny girl was struggling with one of the older girl's bags. It was almost as big as she was. She giggled and bowed her thanks so energetically that Viktor couldn't help but laugh out loud. Viktor moved to take the bag but was interrupted by one of the older girls.

"You no like to talk to me? You no like to help me up on big smelly horse?" She batted her eyelashes and deliberately showed a generous portion of leg as she placed her foot in the stirrup.

Viktor set down the bag, took her by the waist, and hoisted her easily up into her saddle.

"Oooh, such a strong man. I feel very safe. You must have big gun to protect us from wild Indians. Yes?"

"Yes, I have a big gun, but I doubt if we'll need it. There aren't many wild Indians left in these parts. And the ones that are left, like Many Wounds here, are my friends. It's the outlaw white men we have to worry about, if anyone."

Viktor now systematically checked and tightened the straps up and down the line of pack animals.

"We're going to be together for the next week or more so I guess we should know each other's names and establish some rules. My name is Viktor. I know Sam, of course." Viktor turned to the girl he'd helped up on the horse.

"My name is Tsu-jen Sheng," adding, when she saw the confused look on the packer's face, "You can call me Jenny. This is my sister Ling-ling."

"Pleased to meet you. And you, little lady?"

"Unimportant slave-girl. No need name," said Sam.

"It's important to me," returned Viktor. "I have to call her something."

"That's Lalu Nathoy," offered Jenny, who seemed to do the talking for herself and her sister, "but we call her Polly. She doesn't speak much English. She just echoes back what she hears like a parrot."

99

Polly had scrambled up on her pony and giggled again when she was introduced.

"Pleased to meet you, Polly. This is my friend, Many Wounds," said Viktor.

"Pleeze to meet you," returned Polly.

"Good," said Viktor. "That takes care of introductions. We'll be off soon. Today will be the hardest. The descent to the Clearwater is steep and will be difficult for the loaded animals. It will be slow and tiresome. We need to reach the valley floor before nightfall. It would be bad if we have to camp on the steep trail. The rest of the trip we'll go until you're tired, setting the pace that is most comfortable."

Sam nodded, without interrupting.

"I need to know where everyone is at all times. So don't wander off. And holler if you start to get left behind. For the descent today I'll lead the way. Sam, if you and Many Wounds will bring up the rear, I think we're ready to go."

Sam looked nervously toward the Indian but nodded his consent. The rain had cleared the air and greened the landscape. Viktor swung his big chestnut horse around and they were off.

The descent to the Clearwater was slow and trouble-some, as Viktor had predicted. The pack mules picked their way delicately along following the lead of Viktor's chestnut. The girls held up well, but by afternoon Sam was showing the strain. He was falling further and further behind so Viktor called for a halt and a brief rest. The girls made themselves comfortable in the shade of a huge fir tree while they waited for Sam to catch up. Many Wounds had disappeared. Viktor wasn't worried. He knew the *te-wat* would show up when he needed him.

Viktor checked the animals, then offered water to the

girls. "The Indians call this tree *Pe-yersh-i-neet,* a friend with many arms to give shelter from rain."

"Ah, a friend for shelter. Yes." Tsu-jen and Ling-ling nodded and smiled at him.

"Purrish-nit," echoed Polly.

Sam groaned as he climbed down off his horse and joined them. "How much further today, Packer?"

"A couple more switchbacks and we'll be able to see the river. Not much further after that. You holding up okay?"

"Old bones. Just call me Old Bones. I have good Chinese medicine for old bones."

Sam pushed himself to his feet again and went to bulging saddlebags on the side of his horse. He took out a long, thin pipe with a tiny bowl at the end and a tin of opium. With shaking hands he filled the pipe and carefully lit it. The girls watched without interest. Viktor had seen empty opium tins lying about the Chinese camp in Warren, but this was the first time he'd seen someone smoke the Chinese candy. Soon a blue cloud was hovering over Chinaman Sam's head and the fatigue lines in his face had blurred. He rocked back on his heels, smiling, content. When Sam put down the pipe Viktor stood up.

"We shouldn't get too comfortable. We still have a ways to go today."

The girls gathered themselves together and Tsu-jen led the now boneless Sam back to his horse.

"Is he going to be all right?"

"Oh yes, Viktor, he be much better now," said Tsu-jen.

As she put the pipe and the opium tin back in Sam's saddlebags, Viktor could see that the bags were crammed full of similar tins. Even in his drugged state, Sam very carefully retied the bags before climbing back onto his horse.

They pushed on. Sam nodded and swayed at the back of the pack train. The girls were feeling rested and so they chattered among themselves. The afternoon shadows lengthened. Faintly at first, then definitely, the sound of the Clearwater rose up to them. The last switchback spilled them onto the valley floor. They made their first camp as dusk fell.

The next three days passed uneventfully. Many Wounds disappeared and reappeared throughout each day's trek. The group settled into a routine—breaking camp shortly after daybreak and traveling steadily until early afternoon, when the girls and Viktor would eat and Sam would take out his pipe. By the fourth day they had found their stride, so Viktor decided to push on later than usual. An eddy of cool air drifted down from the peaks that lined the Clearwater, bringing a tang of wood smoke to his nostrils. Across the river and through the trees a flicker of light showed in the gathering darkness. The nicker of a horse floated over and Many Wounds appeared out of the forest with his hand raised in warning.

Suddenly an arrow flew out of the darkness and under the feet of Chinaman Sam's horse. Another arrow slammed into a tree an inch from Viktor's head. Two arrows simultaneously pierced the neck of the lead mule, which reared up screaming. Ling-ling, unseated, dropped the reins of her horse and turned to run, but her hand somehow got tangled in her harness. Viktor quickly jumped down and shook her free, then rolled for cover, taking the hysterical girl with him into the lee of the fallen mule.

Now the surprise was over, gunfire began, a succession of shots from the hill across the river. Chinaman Sam let out a yell. Many Wounds had disappeared again.

"Fort up!" Viktor shouted. "Jenny, pull your horse in over there. Take cover. Tie her so she can't break lose." But Tsu-jen stood frozen, unable to move in her terror. Without hesitation Polly grabbed the reins of the older girl's horse and pulled the horse and Tsu-jen into cover.

"Sam, get your gun ready and lay out extra ammunition. They'll rush again in a minute or two."

Polly was the best of the lot, Viktor thought. She had quickly secured her and Jenny's horse and led Tsu-jen to a position behind a big cedar. Just beyond her, Sam frantically tried to free his gun and his saddlebags from the side of his bolting horse. Another arrow flew through the dusk to sink harmlessly into the carcass of the fallen mule. Viktor searched the hills in hopes of seeing some movement that would give him a target, but he saw nothing. Where was Many Wounds?

Clutching his precious candy, Sam ran into the trees. His horse bolted into the darkness as he began to fire blindly into the timber, but Viktor shouted at him to hold off. At least he took his gun, Viktor thought.

"Whoever they are, they're well entrenched. It looks like this ambush was planned." Viktor growled, with a sidelong glance to see how the girls were holding up.

"For sure they mean to kill us!" wailed Ling-ling.

"They've only shot animals so far, but that could just be an accident." Viktor laid out spare cartridges. "We'll find out soon enough."

Viktor considered the situation carefully before making any move. "I'm thinking there's three places where they can get up close enough to do damage. There's that clump of willows along the river, the cedars in the draw to the front of us, and the gulch that swings close just opposite the willows. I'll cover the willows. Sam, you'd better keep an eye on the gulch, and the girls can sing out if they see movement in the cedar clump."

They settled in to wait for the renegades' next move. As Viktor watched the willows, a legend Many Wounds had told him of a young brave desperately in love with an Indian maiden from another tribe came to mind. The girl loved the brave, too, but their tribes were at war. They would meet secretly. One night a warrior from her tribe followed the girl as she stole into the night for her secret rendezvous. While she waited in the darkness for her lover the warrior stole upon her and began to take her by force. Her lover stumbled upon the violent act and drew an arrow to kill the attacker. His jealous rage had blinded him and instead of killing his enemy the arrow penetrated the heart of the girl. When he saw what he had done the brave felt such grief that he fell upon his own knife. Hunyahwat was so moved by the tragedy of the young lovers that he turned them into willow trees—arms forever bent in grief, forever weeping.

Viktor watched the willows and Many Wound's words came back: "She who brings great joy may also bring great sorrow." Viktor shook off a premonition of doom.

The lull continued, and in the silence a swell of nesting night birds flung themselves out of the willows and into the night sky. Meadowlarks.

Viktor took the warning with silent thanks. "They're closing in."

The gunfire began again. This time from the willows.

Viktor had been right. No arrows, though. Then, busy reloading, he spoke with assurance he wasn't sure he felt.

"They still haven't shown themselves. There's not more than three of them. Maybe only two. It looks like they just want to pin us down."

But why? Viktor asked himself. He scanned the willows. Tsu-jen and Polly cowered behind the cedar. Ling-ling trembled beside him. Chinaman Sam, the farthest back, wildly fired off another round. With the last of the light the gunfire petered out again. Ling-ling began to cry.

"What we do?"

"We wait."

On the wings of the larks the night had dropped her velvet nightdress over the mountains. Time stopped and the little group moved toward that place of deepest darkness between sunset and moonrise, when the mistress of the night reigns. An owl hooted. The wind sighed through the trees. The river ran past—black. No gunfire broke the spell. They huddled, breathing shallowly, eardrums stretched taut as the night came awake.

Still no gunfire and no arrows. But Viktor's prickly skin told him it wasn't over yet.

They waited.

Sam's adrenaline and his afternoon smoke were wearing thin. He stealthily shifted through his pockets and filled his pipe, then struck a light.

"Put that out!" hissed Viktor.

Sam quickly extinguished the match, but not before lighting and drawing deeply on the pipe. Polly and Tsu-jen huddled under their cloaks. Viktor crawled over to one of the tethered animals for a blanket to cover Ling-ling. The darkness continued to deepen. Sam sailed away in an opium dream. Viktor listened and waited. The girls, exhausted by the ordeal, gave into the quiet and fell asleep.

Just before moonrise they came. A shadowy figure stepped out from the forest with a flaming arrow raised to the sky. Viktor got off a shot, but the arrow was launched into a clump of dry grass near the cedar and the sleeping girls. Ling-ling cried out as Viktor snatched her blanket away and snuffed the fire.

Sam started awake just in time to see a gun butt come down hard on the side of his head. He crumbled soundlessly.

Viktor squinted through the darkness to see a shadow disappear into the underbrush carrying Sam's saddlebags.

It was over.

Everything fell into place for the packer. The Chinese Candy! That's what they were after. Well, they had it now. Let them be gone with it. The Chinaman's loss. Fool thing to bring it so openly into the frontier anyway. He was lucky he'd kept it this long.

Viktor knelt and examined the lump on the Chinaman's head. He'd live. Probably didn't even feel it, he was so drugged.

They camped where they were.

The next morning Viktor checked the damages. One dead mule and a wounded horse he'd put out of misery the night before. The girls were scratched up a bit, but none the worse for wear. The big loss was the lead mule. Many Wounds turned up at daybreak bringing Sam's missing horse with him.

Chinaman Sam snatched the reins of his horse out of the hands of Many Wounds and said, "Why no Indian helping in trouble last night?"

Unperturbed by the Chinaman, Many Wounds simply said, "This fight was none for me."

"A curse on all the gods. My *joss* is broken. No more luck." He wailed over the loss of his saddlebags.

Viktor interrupted. "We'll be at my homestead in two hours. Can you make it until then?"

The Chinaman didn't answer. He was still cursing feebly in his native tongue when Viktor's homestead came into view.

CHAPTER FIVE

URING THE Vinegar Man's tale you had sketched continuously. First Mary and Corey, sitting close on the rock, and then the Vinegar Man. As his story continued to unfold your drawings of him began to change and it was Viktor the mountain man who began to gaze back at you from the pages of your sketchbook—and Melissa as you imagined her to have been and Polly and the old *te-wat*, Many Wounds. Then, as the story wound down, you returned to sketching Corey once again.

The Vinegar Man came close and gazed for a long time at your drawing of Corey. Corey and Mary came close too.

Marveling, Corey said, "I don't look nothing like that."

"Ah, but you do," said the Vinegar Man. "Clinton draws with his heart as well as his hand, in the manner of a dreamer. He has a great gift from Hunyahwat. With his gift he shows you as you appear to him. A glimpse of yourself you can have no other way. His picture tells me many things and has great power, for we become what we are perceived to be. Clinton sees you as a warrior and a protector, and so this is what you may become."

With these words the Vinegar Man gave your compulsion to draw a dignity you'd never felt about it before. He ennobled what had been furtive. Not just the drawings but your feelings for Corey as well. There was a soft light in Corey's eyes you'd never seen before as he looked at you and back to the picture again.

The Vinegar Man saw it, too.

"You boys remind me of Peter Klinkhammer and Charles Shepp. They fit together like finger and thumb. Peter met Shepp in the Buffalo Hump area back in 1902. Pete had blue eyes and was lean as a lizard, like Corey. They formed the Hump Brewing Company and made two batches of fine beer before realizing the ephemeral prosperity of the boom. Shepp was quiet, like Clinton, with auburn hair. He would make beautiful carvings out of cedar. To watch him work was like watching magic. In his hands, his carvings were alive. When he set one down, finished, it seemed to sleep—waiting for whom it had been made. Shepp told me that he always had a specific person in mind when he began a carving—even if it wasn't a portrait. Most he made for Pete, I think.

"They tried working the mines at Gospel Hump for a while before settling on a ranch across the river from Charlie Bemis and Polly, where they raised a few sheep and made beer. They were friends to the Indians, who had a name for men like them—*Welweyas*. They watched over Polly after Charlie was gone. They were inseparable and died within a week of each other."

The Vinegar Man had taken your sketchbook in his hands. He turned to the picture of Melissa and tenderly touched it, a feathery caress.

"If you boys are camping out, there's a magic place not too far from here you should try to find. A place where the earth still laughs. Do you know where Clear Creek falls into the river?"

"Yes," said Corey, "I think. About a mile up isn't it?"

"Yes. That's where you have to cross over. The Indians used to gather at the confluence and the *te-wats* would journey on alone. They said you had to be pure in heart to find it. Knowing where to cross the river isn't enough. Pete and Shepp knew about it. The Indians told them. Melissa and I went there once. It was the most beautiful place. The last time I was there it was with Many Wounds. That was a long time ago. I haven't been there since." He went muttering away for a moment then looked hard at us.

"But you boys. Follow the creek until you come to the falls. The path cuts behind. Don't look back until you come to an open meadow at the top. You'll know it because it will be filled with yellow flowers this time of year." He handed back your sketchbook. "They say if you don't look back until you get to the meadow at the top you'll get your wish. Beyond the open meadow you'll find two pools—one dark, in the shadows, the other clear. Drink from the first and bathe each other's hands and necks in the second and you will always remember each other.

"After the pools, look for a sentinel, one who watches and guards the way. You'll find it, if you're supposed to. The salmon are running strong this year. They'll show you."

Mary spoke then. "It's true. They told me the way. Go, go. You should go." Laughing, she scooped water and bathed her wrists and arms. Then solemnly came to place her water-cooled hands at the back of Corey's neck. He smiled and shuffled his feet, as was his way, then turned to look at you.

"What do you think, Clinton? Climbing the falls won't be easy."

Without hesitation you said, "Let's go."

You gathered up your things, and the Vinegar Man, like Prospero, waved you away and then called out as you reached the bend in the path. "Don't look back until you reach the top! Watch out for unexpected dangers. This is no ordinary journey you take. It is the route taken by the *te-wats* on many of their Vision Quests. Go carefully!"

So, like two of Lot's followers, or Orpheus and companion, you set out through a gathering mist. Unseen behind you, the Vinegar Man raised his hand, touched his forehead and then pointed toward the sun. His wild gray beard and the staff he leaned on gave him the appearance of Jeremiah or some other Old Testament prophet.

Mary turned again to her cherry picking. The Vinegar Man lowered his arm. The intervening trees quickly obscured you from their sight. The path clung to the river edge then climbed away as cliffs rose and the blue-green water quickened below.

In your mind's eye the image of the Vinegar Man's arm raised to the sun followed you. A shaman's epitaph. A place where the earth still laughs, a sentinel, a field of yellow flowers. Follow the salmon.

Once you crossed the river and came to Clear Creek the valley mists began to give way to the late afternoon sun, the stream spilling out and down, the overgrown path spilling up. One, then the other, appearing and disappearing through the trees before us.

You stepped in Corey's footsteps, effortlessly matching his longer stride from stone to stone, Jonathan following in the shadow of King David.

"What will you wish for?" Corey paused without looking back.

"I don't know. A happy ending, I guess. Or three more wishes."

He laughed easily and moved on. His laughter echoed through the mountain valley like a song.

Then out of nowhere a dream of several nights before came rushing back. At first dimly, then more persistently, until you could clearly remember your dreaming self walking along a hedge of rose bushes, weighted down with an abundance of voluptuous blossoms.

White and pink. In passing I reached out and grasped a large bloom, crushing the petals as I tried to pull it away from the stem without breaking stride. At first it seemed it wouldn't come free, then did. The petals trailed behind me, but I didn't look back as I walked on. Then, as dreams do, it seemed to shift ahead and I found myself lying down, trying to cover my dreaming self with dozens of such petals—soft, thornless, smooth. Then suddenly, the Ghost from the house appeared, knelt above me, and began wiping away the petals. In some supernatural struggle I tried to cover myself and he would remove them just as quickly. I felt his callused hand on me.

You had a distinct dream memory of how the rose petals felt on your stomach and the inside of your thighs.

I remember I rubbed them there, in the dream, even as the Ghost tried to push my hands away, and a musky odor rose up. Not like flowers at all.

Waking, you had wept.

You returned now from the daydream of your night dream to find the mist had gathered again like a shroud to block the sun. A cold stone turned over in your chest, wrenching. From where came this grief? How to make this cold stone melt away and reform into a heart. A bitter yearning welled up from the memory of your dream.

Hidden in the clouds Caseopia and Persedes, Castor and Pollux, the Seven Sisters, spun above us unseen and delirious. The trail took a steep climb heavenward, the mist descended, and we walked toward the clouds, which gathered into a shepherd following two cottonball lambs and a ewe.

"Oh it's up there all right," the Shepherd said quietly, when he came close. "Look for a sentinel. Sleep in the stand of aspen on the far side of the meadow and let the trees whisper their dreams to you. If they should, you'll have found the way."

And he was gone, tumbling after his sheep into the mist below us. Then out of the fog came another man, tall and lean, with smoldering blue eyes. He smiled at us but said nothing, following his friend down the mountain path.

The temptation to turn and look after them was enormous, but you resisted, remembering the Vinegar Man's promise. Besides, the fog was making the rocks slippery and you had to keep your wits about you for fear of losing your footing. The gorge had narrowed and the treacherous path now swung close to the rushing stream. Corey had momentarily vanished, but his voice came floating back.

"The waterfall is just ahead . . . "

The sound of the falls masked anything further.

Slowly, a magical metamorphosis had been taking place in the fog-filtered light. The division between earth and sky had been lost, along with the horizon, in the mist. The path upon which you walked cut through this mist like a ship leaving a wake at sea. The waterfall and sky and mountainside, all the visible world, had been transformed, with the winding path becoming a tenuous thread—the only thing that kept you earthbound.

As you passed behind the silver veil of the waterfall the awful beauty of it was overwhelming. Behind the falls, sounds hung in the air as if you existed in a translucent bell, where that which was far off sounded near, and that which was near sounded as if it could be coming from anywhere. You felt intensely alive, lightning struck with astonishment.

And now the most mysterious thing of all. As you came to stand beneath the silver canopy of the waterfall you had the sense you were standing beside yourself and the line between your waking time and your dream time blurred and changed places in the fertile air. In this altered state, a gathering of figures, both light and dark, slowly materialized—separated from you only by the falling, silvery veil. Your presence had awakened something there and a procession of souls began to pass, like a revelation, through the falling water.

First there were two welcoming shepherds, one tall and lean with blue eyes. The other, shy, had dark-red hair and carried a small wooden carving in his hands. Then came a tiny Chinese woman followed by a quixotic, pear-shaped man with a lofty, harmonious laugh that seemed to ring inside your head. A lovely singing preceded the next figure and a beautiful woman carrying a baby stepped through.

The light figures were separating from the dark and passing. Curiously, you weren't frightened. They seemed real. As if they had always been there and would always be. You were the one that seemed ephemeral.

The curtain parted again and an aged but majestic Indian appeared. He gently offered his hand to a woman and two children in succession. They, as had all the others, sailed up the path and out of the shelter made by the waterfall and the outcropping rock. Ships sailing through time, they disappeared into the fog. Only the old Indian remained between you and the dark figures not yet revealed. He stood for the longest time as if guarding an entrance and looked into your soul seeming to whisper all the while . . .

"He who brings the greatest joy may also bring great grief."

At his words the dark figures, still veiled, churned in anticipation.

He whispered on. "Two in the dark, with a light, who whistle, need have no fear."

"Where am I?" you whispered back.

"Between."

"What should I do?"

"Weave your magic well. Two with a candle need have no fear" was once more his gentle admonition, and he was gone.

And now a command from another place, dark and twisted, without light, but equally powerful enveloped you.

"Reach out your hand," it commanded urgently.

So you did.

The cascading water was an icy razor on your arm. Then something even colder, something dead, grasped your hand and your feet were jerked out from under you and you were falling. Dim, grasping shapes hurled you toward the pool just below, deep at the center, quick and frightening at the edge, where it fell into the precipice.

Suddenly your fall was arrested by another hand, a familiar one.

"Clinton! Are you all right?"

It was Corey. He helped you sit up. Like winged ghosts, the remnants of your vision floated away. Night had fallen and you found yourself sitting up at the edge of the first pool below the waterfall.

"I saw you slip. But you didn't slip." He lit a candle then teased into flame a pile of sticks. "What happened?"

More to yourself than Corey: "They appeared to be the same that we saw earlier on the trail. How could this be? They were welcoming me—us."

"What are you talking about?"

"I was Between."

"Between?"

"Where is my sketchbook? I saw them Corey. I saw them."

"Who, Clinton?"

"Shepp and Pete. They do fit together like finger and thumb. Charlie and Polly, I saw them too. And Many Wounds and Melissa. She carried a baby and was singing. Here, look."

You retrieved your sketchbook from where it had fallen unharmed near the edge of the pool. It fell open to the pages filled earlier with the Vinegar Man's memories.

"There. It was them!" You tore through the pages of the sketchbook excitedly. "They came walking out of the waterfall!"

"Wow, Clinton. You have one vivid imagination!"

You stared into the candle Corey had placed on a rock and whispered, "Two with a light need have no fear."

"What did you say?"

"That's what he told me—Many Wounds. 'Dark grasping shapes seldom will attack two with a light. If they match their strides and whistle.' And here you are with a candle and they are gone."

"Who is gone?"

"The dark ones, from Between, who tried to pull me into the precipice." You paused, flashing again on the beginning of your dream—or whatever it was. "Corey, Shepp and Pete—?"

"Yes?"

"They look like us."

Corey silently stood and climbed up the slippery rocks into the cave behind the waterfall. He returned a moment later. In his hand he carried a tiny, exquisitely carved figure.

"Corey! My god! That has to be one of Shepp's. Where did you find it?"

"Where he left it, I guess.

"The Vinegar Man was right. He warned us. This is no ordinary journey we take."

"Do you want to go back?"

"No. Do you?"

"No."

"Maybe this is the sentinel he told us to watch for, Corey."

You took the tiny carving from his hand and turned it

over and over, marveling. "Somehow I don't think so. For some reason, I imagined something bigger. Something . . . you know, bigger."

"Something imposing."

"Right. I think this is just to let us know were going the right way."

"Yes, Corey. And that someone or something is watching over us."

"What should we do now?"

"I don't know. Wait, let me think. What else did the Vinegar Man say? And the shepherd we passed. What did he say?"

"Don't look back."

"Right. We may have failed on that one. I don't know. Does falling through the falls count? I guess there's no way of knowing."

"Until we make our wishes at the top that is."

"But first we have to find an open meadow filled with yellow flowers."

"And two pools. One dark and in the shadows, the other clear."

"Yes, and we're to drink from the first and wash our hands and necks in the second."

"Each other's arms and necks," corrected Corey. "Do you think it has to happen in that order?"

"I don't know, Clinton." You went on. "We haven't found the meadow yet, but this pool is dark. Do you think we should drink from it?"

"It can't hurt." You placed Shepp's carved talisman in the sand at the water's edge. Corey took the candle and, cupping its flame, placed it down in front of the icon. Then slowly, simultaneously, with gazes locked until the last minute, the two of you bent and placed your lips on the dark surface of the water and drank.

Nothing happened.

You pulled back and your breath went out with a sigh. Suddenly you were exhausted and cold.

"Let's get some sleep, Corey. We'll figure it out in the morning."

You rolled out your bags on opposite sides of the little fire and climbed in—removing only your shoes. The fire died down and the darkness closed in. The end of your bag was wet. It began to soak through your socks. You started to shiver. Somehow Corey knew.

"Are you cold?" he said, an island in the darkness. The fire had been reduced to a few coals. You said nothing, trying to control your shivers.

"Hell, you must be. That bag is dripping. Why didn't you say something? Come over here."

"I'm okay."

"Get over here."

It was an order. You lay freezing for a bit, but his command hung in the air between you. Finally you went picking your way in your socks to where he reclined large in his bag. He threw open his bag to make room for you then, when you hesitated, he pulled you down to him tightly within the curve of his lean belly. Part of you wanted to resist, but the warmth coming off from him was like a lullaby and you began to thaw.

"Getting warm?"

"Yes, a little," you mumbled, resting your cheek on your hand.

He started to curl around you, then yelped, "Your socks are wet!"

"Sorry. Here, let me take them off."

Then after a moment he said, "It's better together, yes?"

"Yes. Next to the best."

And you were asleep.

❀

You slowly came awake cradled by all the earth. The bag was still warm where Corey had been. Some memory lingered of his hand on your forehead while you slept. "The waking I couldn't bear, if in waking you weren't there." You looked up quickly, terrified that he might be gone.

Corey was kneeling at the lip of the falls, a flower growing in a fissure. His face was turned away. You watched him for a moment before he knew. He was so still he seemed of another species. Some animal or plant— some geographic formation that had built up there over the ages.

Maybe from shyness, maybe from contentment at spending the night in each others tangled limbs, we went the whole day without speaking. Whatever the reason, we resumed our quest in silence. We found the meadow. We drank from the shadow and bathed in the light. That night we dreamed our dream in the aspen grove. We followed the path of a scarred and stubborn sentinel. And we didn't look back. We joined the procession. We fell in reverent step. We saw the creator in the creation that day. We became dreamers. We found our *Pe-yersh-i-neet*, our place of shelter—in each other.

The *te-wat* had passed his dreams to Viktor. Your drawings were a sign the Vinegar Man should bequeath his to you. He had sent us to walk where Many Wounds had walked, where Pete once watched Shepp in stillness. Our only voice that day was to speak the names of those who came before us like skipping stones. Our footsteps traced our portraits there in the path with theirs.

There was something indescribable that happened when we stepped out into the open meadow after walking through the old forest all morning. It was physical what we felt, in that shift from the cool mysterious dimness of the forest with its subtle eddies of air wafting smells and whispers into the bright, flat-out joyous light of the open meadow and its rush of air.

The door opened. The temperature changed. We entered another world. We gasped and marveled that two such great beauties existed side by side.

Mystery and illumination holding hands.

The meadow grass stirred like a girl arranging her skirts. The trees, a cathedral entrance, watched at her hem.

How many people live and die nowadays never having slept the night outdoors under a tree or bathed in a lake alone? We did these things, and it did something to us. Now we must sing sad songs for what we had and lost—in harmony with Viktor and Many Wounds.

You saw all the visible world so clearly that day, as if it were freshly carved by a sculptor.

When you came out of the forest, a fox bounded away before Corey through the flower-filled meadow. Where it disappeared, a majestic elk raised its head, herald to a scarred and stubborn giant of a tree that waited, sentinel, across the way. The elk tossed its great antlers, beckoning to us. At the foot of the tree it guarded, nearly hidden in the undergrowth, lay two figures intertwined—lovers carved in stone. When the two of you saw the figures, you looked at each other and walked no more that day.

You found the pools. As the Vinegar Man had promised, the first was dark and in the shadows and the second in the light and warm. Still without speaking, you drank from the dark pool and removed your clothes to bathe in the second.

Silently, gently, you cupped water and anointed the back of Corey's neck. He offered you his wrists. The water glistened on his skin like sparks struck off flint. You felt him and smelled him. He held you close when it was his turn to baptize you. He didn't stop with your neck and wrists but continued up your arms and across your chest, then down your back until you were intoxicated with the nearness of him. His innocent touch erased the dream memory of the Ghost's rough hand. He was in your head, your heart, your hair—this man you had come to love as suddenly as one starting awake from a flash of lightening.

As I look back now I realize it was the only time friendship came first for me, then love. Maybe that's why it was so important. Why it still haunts me. In later years, desire always came first and love came chasing after, never quite catching up, as if some suffocating shroud were among the gifts she brought and, like Jason in Medea's net, I feared I'd be strangled in her web if ever I did allow myself to be faced and chased and caught by love.

We made camp in the aspen grove nearby. Your sleeping bag had dried in the morning walk so you found no excuse to sleep together that night. Without knowing why, you were desolate as you entered your dark dreams alone.

As I fell to sleep that night, I changed wills. For the first time, I wholly took up my other self, my dreamer self. Conscious thought grew falcon wings and I fell into that twilight where certain things are visible that cannot be seen in strong light. Sleep was no longer a passive thing where the body simply recovers, but had become also an instrument of investigation into the unknown—sometimes frightening, always profound.

I dreamed a fire was burning low, on the ground. Those That Walk, one by one, materialized and sat in a circle around the fire, waiting. Then, framed against the sky in the red glow of the flickering flames, Many Wounds appeared and began to move rhythmically. His bone ornaments clattered as he danced and sang. Those That Walk watched in the dim light, their attention riveted on the te-wat's every move. I watched, too. The shaman's excitement communicated itself to us. We knew one another. Our names were written on each other. Smoholla, the Indian prophet, Many Wounds, Viktor—the one who wins. The Welweyas—Shepp and Pete, who had no shame at being halfman halfwoman when they were apart because together they were the best of men. There was Melissa, who sang. Polly and Charlie, who were friends. Those That Walk.

Drawn together by the moonlight and the firelight, the hypnotic rhythm of invisible drums wafted us irresistibly away. The energy mounted until it seemed to burst, shooting like a blazing comet from one of us to the next, until all were in delirium. Then, on a heartbeat, the drumming stopped and in the silence Many Wounds began to sculpt a parable with his dance in the air.

Like a blacksmith with hammer and anvil he slowly reformed himself into a humpbacked white man carrying a child. There was an act of violence. In his dance the shaman circled the fire and the child grew tall with an arrow thrust through his chest. The wound did not bleed. And now, as Many Wounds danced, he became the child. And the arrow was a great rod, and Many Wounds, the child now grown, drew out the rod and struck himself, the father, down.

You woke in darkness to forest murmurs and fell asleep to dream again.

The next day you tried to describe your visions to Corey.

"A dark figure was drawing a picture in the sand of an animal he intended to hunt. He fired an arrow into its throat. I tried, but couldn't see what he'd drawn, then killed in the sand. I had the sense the dark figure was Greegar. I also dreamed a child pulled a rod out of his chest and killed his father, who had put it there. I watched with Those That Walk."

Corey was troubled by your divinations but seemed reluctant to speak of it.

"The Place Where the Earth Still Laughs" was turning out to have some disturbing undercurrents.

You drank from the dark pool, bathed again in the light, and made your wishes before starting back down the mountain. You paused at the waterfall on the return and it seemed as if there was a music there in the cascading water, an airy exaltation of lovely voices. You smiled to hear it. It seemed the two of you no longer walked alone.

The twinkling river and its valley lay just below. You spilled toward it, feeling as if you were being accompanied by Those That Walk. They left you at the valley floor.

The troublesome aspect of your dreams returned with their departure, underscoring the remainder of your homeward journey. What did it all mean? What was the prey Greegar slew in the sand? Who was the child Many Wounds had danced? What was the significance of the arrow and the rod?

Your mother had a kind of sight. Once she said to you at breakfast, "Be careful. Last night I dreamed you broke your back."

You were sitting around the round, red table in the kitchen and you could see she was distressed. It was a Saturday and Dad had taken work cleaning a laundromat on Saturday mornings. You went with him that day and drank bleach from a 7-Up bottle you thought was filled with soda pop.

You couldn't breathe or cry. Your lungs could neither take nor give out. As the room blackened, you went stumbling for your father, frantic, choking, unable to make a sound. He could do nothing as he watched your face turn blue and patted you helplessly until, by magic, the air came back. You gagged and tried to throw up, but couldn't speak to explain.

Later, back at home, your mother had said, "The minute you left I distinctly heard a voice within me say, *Send for him back, something dreadful is going to happen!* At the same time I was seized by a violent trembling and a terrible fear."

Her dream had been a warning, a premonition.

What was yours?

Mary came out to meet you as you passed Rivertown on the way home.

"Hi, Corey. Hi, Clinton."

"Hi, Mary."

The Vinegar Man's hummingbird hovered in the air above her, then darted away when you came near.

"Did you find them?"

You looked at each other. "Yes, Mary, I guess we did."

"I thought so," she said. "You look brighter."

She performed a little two-step in the river road, her bare legs flashing in the sun.

"Greegar came looking for you, Corey."

Corey's face was suddenly like thunder.

"He says he's got work for you to do at home."

"Thanks for the warning, Mary."

"You're welcome," she said, and ran off toward Rivertown. The Vinegar Man's hummingbird, like a guardian angel, appeared and flashed away after her.

"Clinton?"

"Yes?"

"Do you think Mary's pretty?" His question came out of nowhere.

"Yes. I think she's pretty. So do a lot of people."

You waited for him to say something further, but he was silent as you continued plodding up the river road.

You came home to an empty house. Mom had left a note saying she had taken Jerry and gone into Grangeville for the day. Your dad was still working the swingshift and so wasn't home either. The house seemed more sinister than ever. As if your Vision Quest had sensitized you even further to the invisible energies lurking there.

As you went up the steps, Corey said, "I hate to, but I better go and see what Greegar wants. If I don't he'll be over here causing trouble."

"Do you want me to go with you?"

"No. I think it's better if you don't."

"Okay then."

Something wrenched inside at the thought of him leaving you.

"I'll take the pickup. I'll try to be back before dark."

"You're the best. I'll see you when I see you."

"Okay, Wild Man. Try to keep your imagination in check while I'm gone. I'll be back as soon as I can."

As he quietly spoke he put one hand to the hair on the back of your neck. You felt wonder that he had come to touch you so without restraint.

"I'd better go," he said regretfully.

Your devotion toward Corey had grown so strong you would have cut off a limb if he had asked for it. You knew Corey wore chains. His face told you that those chains tightened again with the simple thought of facing Greegar. The darkness of his heart cast a shadow that embalmed your own and you watched him turn to go with great trepidation.

CHAPTER SIX

THERE WAS a Chinese funeral winding its way down Main Street the day Viktor and his passengers got back to Warren.

Chan Lee, a solemn figure, led the way with his hands clasped behind his back. He nodded as the procession passed the new arrivals in front of Bemis's hotel. Chinaman Sam nodded back, still upset over the loss of his Chinese Candy.

The mourners burned punk sticks and strew confetti in the wake of the coffin, which contained Sing Chow, one of the first of the Chinese ever to settle in central Idaho. The incense was burned for luck. The paper punched full of holes was thrown to delay the progress of the devil, who supposedly followed along behind, hoping to possess the soul of the dead one. The devil was thought, by the superstitious Chinamen, to be a snake that had to crawl through the holes in the confetti before he could get to the corpse. So it was hoped that, if buried quickly, the devil wouldn't have time to possess the dead one's soul and the spirit of the departed would be safe.

The Celestials always used shallow graves in Warren, because later the bones would be dug up, ground to powder, and shipped back to China to be laid to rest in sacred ground.

It was terrible bad luck for a Chinaman to sleep in a house where anyone had died. So when Sing Chow fell ill he was carried outside for his dying breath.

Over the past year the rush of Chinese had changed Warren. They had turned out to be the best placer miners of all. They worked day and night, were frugal, kept to themselves, and prospered where many whites had failed. Their success with previously worked claims was a source of discontent to a lot of the lazy white men. The Celestial's foreign ways didn't help matters.

The confetti and burning punk sticks gave the funeral procession a holiday feeling and seemed more like a welcoming committee for Viktor and his pack train than any wake for the dead. Chinaman Sam saw the funeral as another bad omen and wagged his pigtailed head in dismay.

Once the funeral had passed on, Viktor set about unloading the pack animals and depositing the Celestial's bags at the front of the hotel. He was nearly finished when Melissa came outside wiping her hands on her apron. Viktor was overcome with shyness.

"Hello Melissa." (How is it possible? She seems even more beautiful than I remember.)

"Hello Viktor," she said smiling. (He seems taller, stronger. I didn't remember he was so handsome, so manly.)

"Your trip went well?"

"A few mishaps, but we made it in one piece," he said, feeling nervous and looking serious. He paused in his unpacking and watched the funeral procession disappear, acutely conscious of her, seeming to have lost the ability to speak. He repeated silently to himself again and again, as he had on his trip, "I pray her beauty will teach my frowns a more beguiling look."

Suddenly Melissa said, "What do you think happens when a person dies? I mean, do you think they're just gone, vanished forever?"

"No, I don't."

"Don't what?" asked Melissa.

"I don't think they just vanish forever. I think they're still here, but in a kind of dream world that we can't quite see. But they know us and remember us just like we do them. Sometimes I think they can see and hear us as well."

"What a lovely idea."

There was a pause then and Melissa stood smiling at Viktor for a long moment, oblivious to those passing.

Then, "Forgive me, Melissa. This is Chinaman Sam, and the little one is Polly. She doesn't speak much English yet." And then, helping the older girls down from their horses: "These lovely creatures are sisters."

"Hello, Melissa. My name is Jenny," said Tsu-jen. "This is my sister, Ling-ling."

"Welcome to Warren. Please come inside. I'll show you to your rooms." Melissa moved aside to let the Celestials enter.

Once he and Melissa were alone, Viktor spoke again. "May I call on you this evening?"

"I'd be honored," she said, equally formally.

She paused then and watched a warming smile spread across his face. Viktor had one of those smiles that could stop a charging buffalo and break a woman's heart, partly because it rarely appeared and partly because it was so simple and sincere and so obviously filled with joy when it did. The fact that the woods and its inhabitants had witnessed it far more often than human beings was probably the best measure of its worth.

"You don't seem to be frowning anymore. Are you trying to beguile me?" she said, responding to his smile, remembering the words he'd last spoken on their first meeting.

Viktor's smile widened, if that were possible, and he said, "If only I could, then there would be two enchanted people in Warren. For you see, I myself am already beguiled." He bowed gallantly. "This evening then."

When the newly arrived Celestials came down from their room that evening the saloon was already packed with excited miners. Viktor was sitting in his usual place at the end of the bar and Melissa hovered nearby whenever she had a free moment. Charlie Bemis was in the thick of another card game with English Dan and a couple of greenhorns. Cherokee Bob was busy getting drunk. The bar was filled with smoke, laughter, and anticipation.

The saloon fell silent when the Chinese girls appeared at the top of the stairs. Chinaman Sam came first, dressed in Western clothes, sporting a gold watch and chain and carrying a large black bag. Ling-ling was on one arm and

Tsu-jen on the other. Polly came last with one hand clasping the banister for support and her head down. She minced along behind with her curious rolling gait on her tiny feet. When she did look up her eyes were dancing sparrows that darted from side to side, missing nothing.

Ling-ling was the beauty of the three girls, having long eyes, a broad forehead, and a firm rounded chin. Her silky, full, raven hair had never been cut. The sisters had whitened their faces to a death-mask pallor and rouged their cheeks with two spots of high color. Their bottom lips were painted in a scarlet tear drop. Blush had been added to the lids of their eyes, which were outlined with kohl. They exhaled heavenly aromas as they moved down the stairs and across the floor. The entire room was held in a trance by their beauty. No one had ever seen anything like it. To the hungry miners they were exotic creatures that had descended from another world, where graces like themselves were nourished on rose petals and scented herbs.

Above their mask-like visage their hair was gathered up from the nape of their necks into an enormous decoration of imitation jewels shaped like flowers and insects. This crown of hair fanned out at the sides and hung down weighted with tassels of pearls.

The headdresses flattered their round faces by accenting the high cheek bones and their fragile necks, so that they looked like spring trees, bowed with blossoms, that had abandoned their roots and floated into the room.

Their costumes were traditional Chinese. Loose jackets fastened at the sides worn over a tunic and pantaloons. But what costumes! Compared to buckskin and calico they seemed the raiment of angels. They were embroidered with flowers and mythic animals, fantastic emblems and symbolic beasts. All arranged in the most lively colors.

Ling-ling's tunic bore a dragon of imperial yellow and flaunted purple stripes at the hem. The characters for the symbols of happiness were woven throughout—double and wedded bliss.

Tsu-jen wore a crested pheasant with twelve ornamental feathers and the Eight Felicitous Buddhist Emblems woven onto her sleeves in gold and vermilion thread.

Cherokee Bob was the first to speak and break the spell their entrance had engendered.

"How about a drink beautiful?"

"Here's a table," shouted another miner.

"Here's a chair," called another.

"How about sitting on my knee?"

"How about sitting on my face?"

The saloon began to jump as the over-eager men vied with one another for the attention of the girls.

The sisters played their parts well, smiling inscrutably amidst the commotion, pretending to be pleased by it all. They gave no single man more attention than another. It was too early for that.

Sam surveyed prospects calmly, a girl seated on each side, Polly against the wall behind. He checked his gold watch. More to show off than to know the time. He removed his hat and handed it to Polly, who held it dutifully in her lap. Polly was dressed simply and her appearance was a stark contrast to the elaborate makeup and clothing of Ling-ling and Tsu-jen. Sam fingered his string tie and checked his watch again. Tsu-jen and Ling-ling nodded and smiled. The piano man struck up a ragtime melody as the miners continued to clamor for attention.

"How about cutting the rug, little lady?"

"Cut rug?" wondered Tsu-jen.

"How about a dance?"

Sam nodded his consent. "For one dance—one dollar!"

The miner put down five. "I'll take the next five!"

Sam wagged a finger. "One dollar. One dance."

And so it went.

Soon Chinaman Sam had a pile of dollar bills and gold dust stacked on the table in front of him. The pile continued to grow as Tsu-jen and Ling-ling changed partners dance after dance. They appeared inexhaustible as well as exotically beautiful.

The card game between Bemis and English Dan and the others began to look more and more appealing to Sam as his pile of money grew. So before long, leaving instructions with Polly to continue collecting the money the sisters were making dancing, he stood and moved over to Bemis's table and asked to be dealt into the game. The greenhorns folded just then and so Cherokee Bob joined the game, too.

Charlie Bemis had a smell about him that night and couldn't lose. And Sam couldn't win. Neither could Cherokee Bob. Charlie quickly took all the sisters' earnings from Sam and emptied Bob's and Dan's money pouches as well.

"Well, how about it boys?" said Charlie. "Are we through?"

It was then that English Dan made his move.

"One more hand, Charlie. How about you, Sam? Are you still in?"

"So sorry. No more money," lamented Sam.

"Well then, what say the winner of this hand gets a free go at Ling-ling."

"No free time with Ling-ling. No good idea. No."

"How about if Bob and I wager these little tin cans here? Will that change your mind?"

Dan nodded at Cherokee Bob and simultaneously they placed two of the stolen tins of Chinese Candy down on the card table.

When Sam realized what he was seeing he gripped the edge of the table until his knuckles were white and his face had turned apoplectic with rage.

Through clenched teeth he hissed, "This is mine. Where you get Chinese Candy?"

"Hold on there partner," returned Dan calmly. "Out here in the wild west possession is nine-tenths of the law."

"You stole. This is mine!" and he began to curse in Chinese.

"Well, if you think its yours, here's your chance to get it back," spat Cherokee Bob, threateningly.

Sam released the edge of the table and looked around for help. When he saw none was coming, he made as if to stand, then slumped back into his chair, resigned.

"Very well. You win hand, you get Ling-ling. I win, I get all Chinese Candy you have."

"Wait a minute. One tin against one poke with the Chinee girl. No more and no less."

"So sorry, cowboy. We play for high stakes or we no play any more. Ling-ling virgin. Worth many tins of opium for one night with virgin Chinese girl."

"Virgin, my ass!"

"Yes, very much virgin. It is true. And not only virgin, but very famous courtesan as well."

"What the hell is a courtesan?" asked Cherokee Bob, licking his lips.

"Ah, watch and you shall see," said Sam smiling inscrutably, and he clapped his hands sharply twice.

At the sound Ling-ling and Tsu-jen quickly left their dancing partners and came to Chinaman Sam's side. The music stopped and the whole saloon crowded around to see what was happening. Even Viktor and Melissa were intrigued, tearing their gazes apart to turn and watch with the rest.

From the bag at his side Chinaman Sam removed a strange instrument with strings that looked like a cross between a banjo and harp. Various other curious musical devices followed. They pinged and chattered when they were revealed. He cleverly arranged them between himself and Tsu-jen into a small orchestra of string and percussion. Once assembled, he and Tsu-jen and Ling-ling began to relate, with a strange musical background, a sad romantic narration of young, dream lovers.

With a sharp ping on the finger cymbals, Sam introduced the players in a sing-song, high pitched, nasal voice: Oh most womanly, auspicious, heaven-blessed, all-nourishing, brightly manifest, calm, perfect, long-lived, worshipful, illustrious, exalted ones, join me now as I begin our tale of woe. Take care, fair audience, when told for first time in tea houses of Peking, this sad tale caused two women to die of grief. We give you fair warning.

Then Tsu-jen began to sing and play the strings in a strange, dissonant musical mode, while Sam struck dramatic accents with the cymbals and bells hanging from his fingers.

The story, interspersed with erotic interludes, began to be danced by Ling-ling using a swath of red silk and a fan.

To begin she stepped back into a space that had been

cleared and turned her back. She disappeared. Then she turned again and her round powdered face hung bodiless in the flickering light. The slash of red silk began to web itself around this pale moon that was her face and she was the maiden in the tale. She turned again. The silk slashed and wove. She became the lover. Then the maiden, then the lover again—until the characters came and went like heartbeats as she bowed her moonbeam face and the silk twirled red.

The music was strange and wonderful and magical. It enlarged and commented upon Tsu-jen's singing and Ling-ling's dancing. At times it was soft and melodious, dissonant and harsh at others.

Ling-ling's dancing was filled with intimate and mysterious gestures, stylized to the point of movement calligraphy, and suggested falling asleep, flying in a dream, riding on a ship at sea, gathering chrysanthemums in a garden, being a chrysanthemum, and did so with perfect illusion.

As the story unfolded, the heroine was visited by a young student in a dream and fell in love. She hid a portrait of herself in her garden, then pined away and died, yearning for him in vain. The lover, wrecked on a ship at sea, arrived at the empty house where she had lived. He wandered through the empty rooms and came to the garden. There he found the portrait and his heart broke, for he had loved the maiden, too, in a dream. The maiden visited him in a vision and instructed him to find her grave and open her coffin. She was revealed to be beautifully alive.

In a series of complications the young student was accused of desecrating a sacred tomb and the maiden was stolen away by an evil merchant. The maiden was forced to marry the merchant and so killed herself in protest and the student died of a broken heart at the news of her death. They were joined together at last in the spirit world.

When the spectacle was finished the tavern was empty of sound for a moment, and then a collective sigh went round the room.

"Beautiful! Just beautiful," whispered Melissa to Viktor.

"Bravo!" shouted Bemis and stomped his feet.

"Damn!" said Cherokee Bob. "That was somethin'."

And the saloon was filled with shouting and clapping. The sisters smiled demurely and took their bows. When the chaos had subsided a bit, Chinaman Sam turned back to English Dan and repeated what he had said earlier.

"You win hand. You get poke with Ling-ling. I win, I get all Chinese Candy."

"Ya, and if I win I'll take the other one," interjected Cherokee Bob.

"Very well. Please to put all Chinese Candy on table."

English nodded to Cherokee Bob and between the two of them they placed a dozen tins of opium on the table.

"There's the candy you want. Now, let's have a closer look at the candy I want." English took hold of Ling-ling's arm and pulled her roughly onto his lap. She struggled briefly, but when Sam snapped his fingers she fell still.

"Deal Bemis. I'm anxious to get upstairs and try this Chinee filly on for size."

One hand, seven-card hi-lo, dealing to the left, winner takes all.

A snake of excitement went licking and darting its way around the table and a hush blanketed the saloon.

Chinaman Sam, in his eagerness to regain his lost opium, and English Dan and Cherokee Bob, in their desire to have a go at one of the Chinese girls, had forgotten one thing—Charlie Bemis was the most dangerous player in the game and he'd been winning all night.

The essence of poker is bluff and Bemis was a master. He played a quiet game, but knew just when to take a chance and when to run a bluff. It was always the greed of the sucker that makes the skill of the master pay. It was the perfect setup for Bemis to clean house.

Before dealing, Charlie stood up to stretch his legs and get a fresh beer. He took his time coming back to the table and the tension mounted. Cherokee Bob drummed his fingers on the table impatiently.

"Deal, damnit, would ya!"

Then a squall blew up. Cherokee Bob raised out of turn, just as English, sitting across from him, was about to push half his share of the opium tins into the pot.

"If you're really raising, fool, then I don't call," said English pulling his opium back.

"What d'ya mean, you don't call? You already called the bet!"

"My bet wasn't in the pot. You bet out of turn! Didn't he?" English looked around for support.

"What is this?" snarled Cherokee Bob with his short temper. "Is this a serious poker game or are we making up the rules as we go along?"

"Speak for yourself!"

Suddenly everyone was cursing and throwing insults across the table; the saloon was chaos. Everything came to a halt when Bemis pushed his chair back and lumbered to his feet again.

"You girls want to bitch at each other all night or do you want to play this hand?"

"Now hold on, Bemis," whined Cherokee Bob. "I never meant nothing. But you saw what happened."

"Ya, I saw . . . nothin'. Now can we get on with it?"

"Very uncivilized," muttered Sam. "High stakes call for polite game."

"Who dealt this mess?" English threw in his two bits.

"Who do you think, asshole?"

"What the hell are we playing anyway?"

"Can I deal again now, or do you to want to whine some more first?"

"All right, already. Deal."

On the first deal it was obvious it was going to be one hell of a game. Everyone's hand looked loaded. English had an ace and a queen showing, and once again bet half of his pile of opium.

The bet went round to Sam, who thought he had no worries because he had one jack showing and two in the hole for three of a kind, and so he called.

Cherokee Bob looked exuberant with his seven, six, and five of clubs, pushing all of his tins into the pot.

This was no surprise because Cherokee Bob had shown himself to be an impulsive player betting wildly and taking unnecessary risks. His huge raise was in character.

The really surprising thing was that, all the way through, the way the cards fell, everyone had reason to stay in the game and keep raising the stakes.

Then on the sixth card an amazing thing happened. English hit a full house of queens. But only two were showing. He was certain he had the best hand, but did not re-raise in order to keep everyone in the game. Bemis had a bad eight of hearts showing and didn't look too happy, but he called. Sam was very nervous about his three jacks, but he couldn't quit now.

Sam couldn't believe his luck when the final card was dealt. He caught the last jack for four of a kind. Looking only slightly disconcerted, Bemis weighed in with a final bet of $200 against the pile of opium tins and the promise of Ling-ling. This tapped the table. Sam thought he had nothing to fear with his four jacks.

English felt the same with his two queens showing and two hidden.

Cherokee Bob, however, was beginning to sweat. Bemis, as always, was unreadable.

Now came the show-down. The rule of the game was no coin for low, one coin for high, and two coins for both ways; and if a player called both, then he had to win outright, not tie, in order to take the pot. Everyone juggled nervously with his coins under the table.

Bemis increased the tension by announcing, "I'm thinking of going both ways." And up came his hand with two coins in it.

"I've got a six-five for the low," he said.

"Six-five what?" demanded Bob. "I'm six-five, too."

Bemis looked at his hole cards before turning them over. "Six-five-four-two-one," he said.

"Shit!" groaned Bob, turning over his six-five-four-three-ace.

Now it depended on the high. Chinaman Sam looked across to Bemis. "So sorry, I've got four of a kind," and he displayed his four jacks.

"Bad luck," said English, grinning triumphantly. "I also have four of a kind—queens."

With a flourish he spread his cards and made a move to embrace the pot.

But then Bemis turned over his cards, showing in the hole six and five and two of hearts.

"I've got a straight flush," he said calmly, not raising his voice by a decibel. Lying there like a message written in stone was four-five-six-seven-eight, all hearts with his ace of clubs and two of spades for the low hand.

"Shit!" shouted English and threw down his cards. "Never have I seen such a hand. A straight fucking flush out of nowhere. Give me a shot of whiskey, Melissa. Make it a double."

Sam had turned pale with the shock of his loss.

"This here game is over," said Bemis. "I don't want Ling-ling or Tsu-jen, but I would like to buy the little one a drink," and he nodded toward Polly, watching wide-eyed against the wall.

Sam, somewhat relieved, took Polly by the hand and led her over to a chair near Bemis. The music resumed and the dancing started up again. Soon Ling-ling and Tsu-jen were taking turns leading miners upstairs at ten dollars a pop. Cherokee Bob and English Dan, having been relieved of all their capital, were of course denied access to the delights of the Chinese woman and their fury increased in direct proportion to their drunkenness.

Bemis, an astute and observant man, had noticed Polly's strange gait and asked her about it and how she had come to be with Chinaman Sam.

Polly, in broken English interspersed with pantomime, began to try and explain.

She was the first of six children, and from the age of five bandages were bound tightly round her feet, forcing the heel under the instep to meet the crumpled toes until the whole foot measured not more than three inches in length. This was done to many Chinese girls of the upper class who would then spend their whole life mincing along daintily on swollen and deformed ankles. This was the famous "lily walk" that caused an undulation of a woman's figure, which in China was considered the height of beauty and seductiveness. The spectacle of a Chinese girl tottering about on her cramped and crippled feet was celebrated in prose and verse, even though, quite often, when the bandages were changed, the stench of compressed flesh was appalling. But bound feet were not only thought seductive, but were also a symbol of caste, for the coolie class could not afford to immobilize their daughters, but urgently needed their labor.

When Polly was thirteen her father was cashiered for deserting his post before the onslaught of the Taiping rebellion. As a result, the family lost its status and Polly's bound feet became a disadvantage. There was no hope now of her marrying into nobility.

For the next two years Polly's family traveled as part of a soup kitchen through the teeming crowds of Peking near the gates of the Forbidden City. The soup kitchen consisted of a fortune teller, who was also a scribe, a beggar priest, a turner, who sold spoons, and Polly's father, who made a meager living shaving men's foreheads in the Manchu style.

Polly's brothers and sisters gathered night soil parsimoniously in jars, for the merchants who collected manure—human and animal—and carried it to the countryside to be used as fertilizer. Their life was squalid and diseased and there were too many children. In the family's reduced financial state Polly had become a liability. So when the opportunity came she was sold.

"My folluks in Peking had no grub. Day sellee me . . . Slave girl. Old woman she smuggle me into Portland. I cost $2,500!" she said proudly. "Old Chinee-man Sam take me along to Warren on pack train."

Bemis shook his head in dismay at Polly's story.

Meanwhile the party atmosphere in the saloon was winding down. The piano man had gotten too drunk to keep a proper tempo and Tsu-jen and Ling-ling had reached the limit of their endurance. So Chinaman Sam called a halt to the trips upstairs.

"Come back tomorrow," instructed Sam to the remaining miners. "Much more good-time tomorrow."

There was a little good-natured grumbling, but they went willingly enough when Bemis, with the help of Melissa, coaxed and half-carried the remaining men outside.

"What a night!" sighed Melissa, exhausted.

"I'll say," agreed Bemis. "How about if we clean this mess up in the morning?"

Sam and his girls retired to their rooms and Bemis locked up. Viktor and Melissa sat for a moment on the boardwalk outside the saloon and counted the stars before saying good night.

"I'll have to be getting back to my homestead in the next day or so," remarked Viktor.

Melissa nodded.

"Would you care to come and see my place?"

"I'd love to. I'll have to let Charlie know. Can you come by in the morning?"

"Certainly."

"Tomorrow, then."

"And tomorrow and tomorrow," he said and he walked away into the starry night.

❀

Early the next morning, while Bemis and Melissa were cleaning up, Sam came down the stairs with Polly on his arm. Sam was trembling from the night's events and his lack of opium and it was obvious he had something on his mind. He shakily took a seat at the bar and Polly climbed up next to him. Polly smiled at Bemis. Her most appealing feature was her vivacious expression and it deepened when her smile flashed with winning suddenness. Bemis smiled back.

"You like Polly?" asked Sam.

"Sure, I like Polly," said Charlie Bemis, puzzled.

"You want?"

"Hold on there a minute. What do you mean?"

"You want. I give."

"Hey, partner. I don't pay for women, and besides, isn't it up to Polly?"

"Not important. You give me Chinese Candy, I give you Polly."

Bemis stared, incredulous, at the Chinaman.

"She good girl. No good for dancing. Too ugly for bed. I lose too much money. She good girl, take care of you, take care of saloon. Good cook. Very much, please, Mr. Bemis, you take Polly, I take Chinese Candy."

Bemis looked at Melissa and back to the Chinaman and Polly, speechless. "What does Polly have to say?"

"I very good cook, Charlie!"

145

"I don't want a wife."

"That okay. I cook. You eat. You get very fat and happy. Yes?"

"Give him the candy, Charlie," said Melissa. "Polly can stay with me. God knows we could use some extra help around here. Besides what are you going to do with a dozen tins of opium?" and then to Bemis, aside, "Think of the life she'll have if she stays with Sam."

"That's true."

"Viktor has invited me out to his homestead and I'd like to go," she said, blushing. "Polly would be a big help around here."

"All right, all right. I never could win an argument with a woman."

Charlie gathered up the opium tins from where he'd stashed them behind the bar and passed them over to the elated Chinaman.

Sam took them with shaking hands and hurried up to his room, leaving Bemis gazing, disconcerted, at the tiny girl perched on the bar stool across from him.

Melissa laughed and said, "It looks like you got yourself a new cook, Charlie."

While Melissa was still laughing at Charlie's bemused face, the saloon door swung open and English Dan entered. Melissa's expression instantly changed and she said, "We're not open for business yet, English. Come back later."

He ignored her and moved over to Bemis as he took out the fixings for rolling a cigarette.

"You see this cigarette I'm rolling here, Bemis?"

"Ya, I see it. So?"

"By the time I've finished smokin' it, I want the money

you cheated me out of last night. And if it ain't here in front of me by the time I'm finished, I'm gonna shoot you in your right eye."

Bemis made a move toward his gun hanging on the wall at the end of the bar.

"Don't even think about it, Charlie," English said, as he pulled out his revolver, placed it on the bar, and lit his cigarette. He took a drag, exhaling in Charlie's face.

"I wouldn't advise calling my bluff on this occasion, Charlie," and he took another drag. "Nobody comes up with a straight flush without cheating. I want my money back, and I mean to have it one way or another."

"You're too stupid for me to have to cheat to win," said Bemis.

Dan's eyes narrowed at the insult and he took a last drag off his cigarette.

"Very well," he said and raised the gun.

Before Charlie could duck or move, English pulled the trigger. Bemis dropped like a felled tree his hands covering his face. Polly let out a scream and Melissa grabbed Charlie's gun out of its holster hanging on the wall. English took another shot at the fallen Bemis, but his gun misfired and he dropped it like a hot coal.

"Now, how would you like to try calling *my* bluff, English?" screamed the furious Melissa. English Dan slowly raised his hands.

"Now, let's see how good you are at dancing out of here, backwards." She fired the gun at the outlaw's feet. He jumped. "Not good enough. Let's try again," and she fired two more shots in rapid succession. "You cowardly snake. How does it feel being bested by a woman?" she shouted as he fled.

Polly and Melissa rushed to the fallen Bemis who lay groaning on the floor. Melissa raised his bloody head. Miraculously the bullet had lodged in the eye socket and the damage wasn't fatal. But the bullet had to be removed. While Melissa held his head, trying to stop the flow of blood, Polly hurried upstairs to her room and came back with a crochet hook. Delicately she inserted the hook into the wound, trying to remove the slug. Bemis cried out in pain and twisted away.

"Charlie, you must hold still or you're going to lose your eye."

"Whiskey," he groaned.

Melissa poured nearly a fifth of whiskey down his throat and Polly tried again. Melissa held his head. On the third try the bullet came free and Charlie passed out.

Over the next few weeks, while Bemis convalesced, Melissa and Polly took over the running of the saloon. Melissa worked the bar, as usual, and Polly did the cooking. Her cooking was good, but her coffee was terrible. No matter how hard she tried, it would end up being too strong or too weak or filled with grounds. But her winning personality more than made up for the inadequacies of her coffee. Viktor got in the habit of complaining goodnaturedly just to see her reaction.

"My God, who made this mud? Someone is trying to poison me!" he would say loudly.

With mock fury, the tiny woman would come running out of the kitchen swinging a gigantic meat cleaver.

"Who no likee my coffee?"

In feigned dismay Viktor would cower in his seat. "Not me, Polly. You know me. I just love your coffee!" and he would raise his cup, take a couple of big gulps and smack his lips, nearly choking.

Polly would watch, scowling furiously, until her victim had finished, down to the last drop. Then she would fill his cup again and return to the kitchen with her rolling gait, a big smile on her face.

Once Charlie Bemis was back on his feet and it was clear Polly had things under control, Melissa took a few days off and went with Viktor to see his homestead.

CHAPTER SEVEN

VIKTOR AND Melissa were coming to fill for each other that awful need every person has to find the center of a safe circle of their own making. Their courtship, their emergent love, the journey to Viktor's were each a part of their closing such a circle. They traveled in a companionable silence the fifteen miles north to the cabin, needing few words. Viktor's love of Melissa, her beauty, her body, her voice, clung to him like a welcome fever.

For Melissa, the air smelled like light and she felt as if she had wandered in shadows, dim and distracted, and now suddenly she had awakened. Time seemed not to pass. When the boundary of Viktor's land came into view he turned to her as if offering a gift.

Straight before them a white-sanded path curved toward a bridge across a creek and up a gentle hill. On either side of the path, flamed foxglove and wild tiger lilies tossed their heads offering nectar to a thousand bumbling bees. On the right, the hill, crowned with majestic pines, dropped away toward the creek. Midway between the foot of the hill and the creek stood the cabin. Flung before it lay a carpet of gold—the face of heaven in a field of yellow flowers.

"Why didn't you tell me it was so beautiful?"

"Until I saw you see it, I don't think I knew."

"Those white star-shaped flowers by the bridge? What are they?"

"Columbine."

"Yes? They look like tiny dancing girls in white dresses."

"They do, don't they."

"And the tall slender ones, over there?"

"Arrowhead lilies."

"You know them all don't you?"

"Not all. But most."

They tethered the horses and crossed the bridge toward the rambling cabin nestled in willows at the foot of the hill. Above, behind, and at the sides, the trees rose in a green umbrella over the cabin. The white-sanded path ended at three steps, introducing a wide covered verandah that lined the front of the house. Graceful vines climbed the verandah toward the roof. Baskets of wildflowers hung suspended from the beams. The effect was wild and wonderful. As if the cabin were the nest of some great forest creature laid gently on the land.

Inside, the floor was of wooden planks, sanded and oiled to a beautiful finish. On the inner wall was a huge bookcase stuffed full of books, beside it an oak desk. Melissa ran her hands along the books, examining the titles. Shakespeare, Dickens, Hawthorne, Milton, their novels and sonnets and plays.

"How did you get so many wonderful books."

"Slowly and carefully, over the years."

She took his hand in two of hers, smiling. He responded by leading her into the next room. It contained two beautifully made oak chairs and an enormous bed. The bed was low, lying next to a large sun-filled window. The thick mattress was filled with hemlock twigs and sweet fern on which the sun shone all day.

In the sparkling sunlight they took off their clothes and stared at one another with a sense of urgent wonder. Melissa stepped closer and tenderly reached up to touch the perfection of Viktor's muscular chest, which was lightly sprinkled with reddish-brown hair. He groaned aloud at her touch and pressed her hands to him. Like water over rocks, spilling, they embraced.

"Melissa?"

"Yes, Viktor?"

"You are the most beautiful creature I've ever seen. Even more beautiful than the red-tailed hawk that rules the sky above here. I never imagined myself saying such a thing to another person." He smiled down at her. "I haven't much experience with women. But if you would consent to be my wife, I would spend my life loving you with every fiber of my being."

"And I, you."

He swept her up into his strong arms then, and laid her gently on the bed. In the sunlight they gazed at one another helplessly, overwhelmed, trying to memorize a mystery.

He touched her lips.

She cupped him gently in her hands.

He traced the curves of her body again and again.

When they could bear no more, they moved apart and lay facing each other holding hands and watched the afternoon sun shift patterns across their flesh. Each play in the light revealed some new and precious place on the other's body, a landscape to be explored, to be kissed and touched and treasured.

It was really that day they married, but they exchanged vows out-of-doors on the outskirts of Warren, with their friends as witness. They were loved by all and the entire community came to the wedding. The clearing where the ceremony took place was filled with rhododendron and daisies. Polly, with Bemis's help, intertwined more daisies in ropes of pine bows and hung them in festoons from the limbs of trees. They chose for their altar a flat-topped stone in the center of the meadow. It was surrounded by lacy fern and lily of the valley.

Melissa had made her own wedding gown of satin and lace with tiny cloth-covered buttons up the back. The day of the wedding she carried a simple bouquet of lily of the valley with green ribbons woven throughout. She smiled a signal to Charlie Bemis, when all had assembled, and he lifted his violin to his shoulder to underscore the vows she had elected to sing. She had practiced her part of the ceremony in private, as had Viktor, so neither he nor she was quite prepared for what the other brought to the ritual bonding.

When she began to sing, Viktor's mouth fell open in amazement, for nothing in a man's capacity to understand could have prepared him for the clear, simple beauty of her voice lifted in love. Nothing. The wind, the violin, meadowlarks, the entire day joined her voice in lovely canticles that celebrated the beauty of their union and the earth. It wasn't just that Viktor listened with the ears of one who loves—a love so perfect he could smell it and taste it and feel it, warming a frozen place deep inside—all who listened were affected similarly. Only those who heard Melissa sing could ever really understand. What they witnessed was so pure, so profound, so moving that it could not be kept in memory and savored. It had to be experienced again and again to be believed. Those who heard her voice that day later swore it was the only one of its kind outside of paradise.

When she began to let loose the full power of her voice, those assembled there found themselves lost in rapture. Melodies turned to liquid fire when passing her lips and washed away loneliness and pain in a deluge of swiftly descending ecstasy. Every note was intimate. The kind of intimacy that reforms two into one.

Viktor into Melissa.

As he listened and watched his beloved, his throat constricted and tears of happiness spilled down his cheeks. No one was unshaken. All were filled with silent wonder and many were found to be weeping when her song was finished. Then through his tears of joy, Viktor took his turn, speaking his promise, in simple tones of quiet humility.

I pray your beauty will teach my frowns a more
 beguiling look.
Enrich my solitude with your presence that I may at
 last be a proper man.
I have been forged and formed by the absence of
love and it is this that has set a stern visage upon

my brow. Now let your proximity reform me into a
    lovely man,
a gentleman, irresistible to the one I desire.
For it is not enough to be a strong man. My strength
can fetch me only trifles.
Let me love and be loved.
Rude seas and certain stars have heard my confession.
Well placed mountain paths, where wild fox glove
    grows,
have born the burden of my sorrowful gait.
Therefore let your beauty teach me companionship,
as it has taught me desire.
Wait on me and lead me to this contentment.
Not taken for the expected nor the granted, but gifted
by chance, thus the more treasured.
To be ever friends.
To spill from my overflowing cup to your bottomless
    well.
To spend the rest, filling and emptying, filling and
emptying, each other again and again and again.
And I pray our love will be ever a mystery, this quick,
bright, thing, ever a mystery.

They had one year together, the kind of year many
people spend a lifetime trying to find. They worked hard.
They prospered. The land blessed them. Viktor continued
his packing trips and Melissa went with him. The winter
was mild that year. At Christmastime they discovered
Melissa was pregnant. By spring, as was to be expected,
their supplies were running low, so Viktor set out for a day
of deer hunting. He was a mile from the homestead when
it started to rain, so he turned back for a heavy overcoat.

The coat is probably what saved him. He set out again. Early on the dogs came upon a fresh scent. They ran down a big buck, driving it out of cover and across the ridge where Viktor could get at it. It was a majestic animal and he bagged it as it stood for a moment on the ridge silhouetted against the morning sky. He was only about two miles from the cabin. He took a single shot and it dropped where it stood. He spent the morning dressing the deer. The dogs foraged intermittently through the underbrush back down the trail.

He had tied the finished carcass across the rump of his horse and started back when the dogs set up a frenzied yelping. He found them worrying a baby cougar they had dragged out of its den. Viktor sensed in the rising hackles at the back of his neck that the mother was somewhere nearby.

He called off the dogs, tied up the horse, and went to retrieve the cougar cub.

He was carrying his rifle in one hand and the cub in the other when the enraged mother launched herself out of a tree, where she had been concealed in the thick foliage. She landed on his back, knocking him to the ground and sending his rifle flying in one direction and the terrified cub in the other. The maddened female cat, scratching and biting, began to rip the overcoat to shreds, quickly tearing through to bare flesh.

Fortunately, he still carried the hunting knife he'd used to clean the deer. With a series of desperate, back-handed thrusts, he drove the knife into the soft underbelly of the cat. He was able to mortally wound the animal, but not before it tore a deep, raking path from his shoulder down to the middle of his back. Bleeding profusely, he managed to crawl back to his horse and climb up in the saddle. The pain was excruciating.

Melissa had heard the screams of the wounded cat echoing down into the valley from the ridgeline trail and quickly saddled up a horse to investigate. Somehow she knew Viktor needed her. She found the dogs first, then her husband, slumped over the saddle of his horse, barely conscious, covered with blood.

Viktor's injuries prevented him from making the first of his usual summer pack trips. By the time he was mended, Melissa had come due, a month early, and he missed the second. Fortunately, the delivery was a simple one. They named the boy Christopher. By the time the baby had reached his sixth week, Melissa knew Viktor couldn't wait any longer. If he did, they would never make it through the next winter with their remaining supplies.

"You must go sweetheart. I'll be fine."

"If only Many Wounds were here. I don't know why he hasn't come round yet this summer."

"That's all the more reason you should go. He'll probably show up here any day."

"I just don't want to leave you alone."

"Someone has to stay and feed the animals. I didn't come all the way here from St. Louis to let a new baby slow me down. I can take care of myself. You're not forgetting who you married, are you?"

He shook his head, worried.

"It's safer for the baby here. The winter's coming fast. It would be dangerous for him on the trail. You must go, Viktor."

And he let her persuade him.

So she sent him into town and stayed to continue the

work they had begun together on the homestead. She had made a gentleman of him and took his will and caring when she was gone. There would be no chance she'd not succeed, not Melissa. So before the first snow touched the mountains ringing their valley, he'd left for Grangeville, out of season, leaving Melissa behind, against his better judgment.

A thin finger of smoke pointed accusingly at the sky, marking their cabin site, when he turned for a last look.

She'd be all right.

"Go," she had said, "go."

So he headed out, pushing the animals too hard, trying to convince himself he was doing the right thing.

"She'd be all right," she had insisted. "Her and the baby."

The last image he had of her standing in the cabin door rose up to blind him.

Goddamn her and goddamn the memory of what he would never ever be able to forget—what he found when he got back to the homestead written in blood on the sheets.

The trip had taken too long. The weather had been warm, unseasonable when he left. But snow had caught him on the way back and delayed his return.

She'd called out his name their last night together, in her sleep, and then again when he got out of bed that morning, letting the covers fall away, as she sat up and smiled at him, so that her white skin stood out sharply against the dark headboard.

"I'll be all right. The motion of my heart will bring you back to me, safe."

Her words echoed after him and became a morbid epitaph for driving his return to the homestead and his family. It rang loudly in his head again when he looked down on the cabin and the smokeless chimney and the pens hanging open. The stark stern terror of what he had feared rose like a dark specter in the aspect of the empty cabin windows.

When he found her, he fell to the floor, his grief a knife through the heart. After a time he crawled up on the bed next to her remains and willed himself to die. But he did not die; instead she came to him in a dream and he relived her last day.

It was one of those warm, Indian summer days, the morning Viktor left. Melissa fed the baby and went about humming to herself as she did her chores. Midmorning, she went outside to work a bit in the garden and to feed the animals. It was when she went into the chicken coop that tragedy struck. Seeking protection from the chill of the night, a snake had hidden itself in the warm straw—a rattler. When Melissa bent to scatter feed to the waiting chickens it struck, its fangs sinking into the back of her leg just below her calf. She kicked the snake away, forcing herself to stay calm. Moving slowly she returned to the cabin for a knife to lance the wound and drain the poison. She twisted around and reached down to make the cut. Too deep. Blood began pouring from the slash. She couldn't stop it. She began to weaken rapidly and she knew she was going to die. The baby would starve! In her last moments of consciousness she gathered the baby into her arms and crawled into bed where only that morning she and Viktor had made love for the final time. With the last of her strength she covered the baby's face with a pillow and held it there, her heart breaking. Then in blood she wrote on the sheets, "Rattlesnake bite, baby would starve . . . "

Three days later Many Wounds found Viktor there, curled around her frozen corpse. A breathing thing, but not alive. The *te-wat* led Viktor gently away, a dumb and unfeeling animal with no will of its own.

To a Dreamer every tree, every river and thicket was inhabited by invisible forces that must constantly be placated by incantations and prayers. Every event had a reason, if impossible to comprehend. Mystery held a powerful grip on all life and fate was often determined by a shift in the wind. What Viktor could not bear would destroy him. He lived like a stone, but he lived, so it was not yet finished and this the *te-wat* knew.

"Life is never ours to own, only a gift temporarily given into our protection."

The *te-wat's* words gave no comfort and Viktor's gulping sobs strangled him.

"I didn't protect her! I left her alone. I failed her. The thing I cherished most I've lost forever. Forever," and he shrank into himself, gnawed by the jaws of inconsolable grief.

Many Wounds led him tenderly away. The Mountain Man did not speak again for days.

Many Wounds took him to a great forest, where no white man had been before, that echoed with a thrilling silence. They passed behind a lovely silvery waterfall and then came to an open meadow filled with flowers. At the edge of the meadow were two pools; one in the shadows—dark—and one in the light. As they came to stand before a magnificent tree between the two pools, Many Wounds paused and made the traditional Indian genuflection, touching his weathered forehead, then caressing the scarred trunk where many hands before had worn smooth a place.

Viktor stared silently at the tree, but made no move to touch it; there was something foreboding in his calculated neglect to give honor.

"They say," Many Wounds prompted gently, "that when a something is broken, *Pe-yersh-i-neet* may offer shelter to the pure in heart. Many who have passed on still walk here, finding shelter."

Viktor turned and with empty face said, "There is no shelter. There is brief beauty. There is music . . . but there is no God and he can offer no shelter."

And he felt silent again.

With no will of his own, Viktor followed where the *te-wat* led. Many Wounds instructed Viktor in the ways of medicine men and he seemed to hear, but the *te-wat* could not be sure.

The old *te-wat* told Viktor, "A healer is not like an ordinary man. He must listen more to his dreams than his physical desires, until it becomes instinctive. Instructions from the spirit world can be dangerous if misunderstood. If a *te-wat* loses his way, he loses his soul. It is good you do not speak. Your heart is in the spirit world, with Melissa now. When it is mended a little, your voice will return to you and your next task will be made clear."

Without seeming to do so, Many Wounds instructed Viktor in the art of setting bones, and how to use cobwebs to stop the flow of blood. Together they gathered herbs and berries that had the power to cure disease.

Soon Viktor was gathering herbs and mixing ingredients on his own, as if he had been born to do so. But still he did not speak and the expression on his face never changed. Each formula was of an exact and correct consistency, which in some cases could have been lethal if mixed improperly. He accomplished these tasks each time without difficulty and without fail. One measure of potent herbs, two of ripened berries, heated to the point of boiling, then cooled before being administered. Simple enough each step of the way, but disastrous if done in the wrong order or incorrect proportions

Even Viktor's first silent attempts were perfect. A wonder and a mystery to Many Wounds. The *te-wat* was startled by Viktor's accuracy and the reverence with which he worked. Perhaps it made him forget his loss a little. It seemed nothing else could.

Over time a slow transformation began to take place. Viktor, who had always been sympathetic to the ways of the Indians, shook off the last remnants of his Christian heritage and began to move through the forest like a deer or some other silent forest creature. It was wonderfully pleasing to watch in a man so tall and strong. It was clear he still carried his grief with him like an open wound. Perhaps he always would.

Some men love only once. Maybe Viktor was such a man. A tragedy to lose such a great love so soon, when his love was still in its first bloom. Day after day, Many Wounds watched Viktor suffer, and a part of him suffered as well.

Although Viktor's remedies were seldom flawed, he was never too proud to accept assistance from Many Wounds if he needed it. Soon, however, Many Wounds realized there wasn't much more he could teach Viktor. He had become a *te-wat* of great power and perception.

The years passed slowly, and one unfortunate day a plague struck the tribe, and the wife of the chief was one of the first to fall ill—deathly ill. Many Wounds tried everything he knew, but to no avail, and turned to Viktor with resignation.

"She is finished," he said sadly. "It is time for her to go."

Viktor raised his eyes, a strange anger filling him at the announcement of the *te-wat*. He was not content to sit passively by and wait for the woman's death song to be sung.

He rose quietly and crossed to the woman's tent. He could see she was suffering greatly. She lay groaning, wrapped in her blankets in the darkness furthest from the fire. In her pain, she was unaware of his entrance and the healing hands he placed on her brow. He began to mix a potion of herbs and berries and then stirred them carefully as he heated the mixture on the open fire. He let it cool, then gently lifted the old woman's head and helped her drink. She slept quietly that night, for the first time in many days. She slept through the next two days as well. When she woke she had recovered.

The student had become the teacher.

The plague began to decimate the Indian camp. Many fled to the Christian mission for help, but were turned away and left to die where they fell, overcome by fever.

Spaulding, the Methodist minister, and his wife, prayed over those who had been baptized, but Jesus had turned his face away and most died.

Those Viktor treated fared better. And the legend of the Wizard of Dreams was born.

The tribe was being strangled by superstition as well as disease, and those who recovered under Viktor's care began to regard him with a sense of awe and fear. They attributed his healing powers to an ability to control unseen forces and therefore a kind of sorcery.

His months of silence only added to his mystery. A lesser man would have taken advantage of their superstition to gain power in the tribe. Viktor was not such a man. He simply continued on his silent way, helping when he could, mourning with the rest when he could not. But for the first time the sharpness of his grief was dulled a little and he began to notice again the world around him.

He no longer had faith in the Christian God, and so it was Hunyahwat he called upon in his prayers.

There was something wondrously magical in the curious ritual he would perform whenever one of his companions would fall ill and then recover. For Viktor it was a simple giving of thanks and he would consummate the act in solitude. But the children of the tribe fell into the habit of following him and watching in breathless wonderment.

He would silently speak the name of the one who had been healed and lift his arms heavenward, as if communicating with some pagan deity. Then he would carve a pattern with his arms, sculpting the air before him again and again.

It was a dazzling and awesome thing to behold.

The mystery of the Wizard of Dreams grew.

Viktor had come to know what many of the Dreamers had forgotten under the corrupting influence of the Christian missionaries—the old ways were best.

The earth had answers white men would never hear, if only because they had never learned to listen—until it was too late.

The old ways were best for anyone with patience to listen and to understand. The white man had brought decay and disease in his wake. His trinkets, his guns, and his machines could not help the Indian, only hasten his destruction, and eventually these same evil devices, disguised as gifts, would destroy the earth.

Soon there would be no *te-wats*. No Dreamers. Viktor had come to know this and took up the mantle. Unwittingly he turned his back on his own people when he turned his back on God—the God that he blamed for taking Melissa from him. In doing so, he began to put some of his grief aside, and his new task, as Many Wounds had foretold, came clear. He was to be a Sentinel of the Earth. One who watches and guards the way. His dreams would be his guide in protecting his adopted people and the land.

Even the animals began to sense his benevolence. He gave away his pack mules, keeping only his beautiful chestnut horse. It followed where he would go like a faithful dog and his homestead began to be filled with forest animals he was nurturing back to health: a red-tailed hawk with a broken wing, a lynx with an infected eye, a lizard without a tail, an orphaned baby marmot. All fell under his protection.

He never used a saddle or a halter on the chestnut, explaining to Many Wounds, "He chooses to carry me. As the raptor chooses to follow me and hunt for me. As these berries and herbs choose for themselves to heal or not to heal."

The *te-wat* thought to himself: "A strange and enigmatic man. A Wizard of Dreams. He has truly become one of the ones who knows. I was right to teach him."

Viktor's wild patients manifested the usual response to strangers, running the gamut from studied indifference to outright hostility. When Many Wounds visited the homestead, he was no exception. But as the *te-wat* watched, they slowly, one by one, left their perches or nests or hiding places in the cabin to come and pay homage to Viktor.

The lynx came first to rub his head against his legs. The red-tailed raptor, long healed, fluffed his feathers and screeched before flinging himself gracefully off his perch to swoop around Viktor's head and back to his perch again. A baby raccoon made a pest of himself, getting underfoot, demanding attention. They acted like pets with Viktor. To anyone else they were wild things and had to be approached with caution or not at all.

The cabin was filled with this assortment of creatures in various stages of recovery so that it was more of a menagerie than a house. And once again it was filled with love.

The only white folks Viktor would spend time with were the *Welweyas,* Peter Klinkhammer and Charles Shepp. They had found the courage to love against tradition and for this reason Viktor felt they understood his grief the way others couldn't. Whatever the reason, he avoided all but the briefest contact with other white men.

Sometimes he would share an afternoon of fishing with Polly and an evening drinking whiskey with Charlie Bemis. In summer Polly's garden was filled with strawberries, watermelon, and vegetables of all kinds. Her plum trees and pear trees would intoxicate the air with the fragrance of their blossoms in spring. While gardening, whenever she would find a worm, she would deposit it in a pocket of her apron and then faithfully, every day at three in the afternoon, she would stop whatever she was doing and go fishing. She was so tiny she was afraid one of the huge salmon she was always catching would pull her into the river.

When Peter and Shepp would come to visit, she would inevitably say to them, "You no catch none today? You no good. You fella come over Sunday. I cook big one I catch today."

Viktor would smile, charmed by her good-natured teasing of the *Welweyas*.

Viktor had always been a born storyteller. When he began to speak again, wonderful legends of the Nez Percé fell from his lips with a hypnotic intensity that was extraordinarily compelling. The deep resonance of his voice was more akin to singing than speaking and had the effect of whispered revelations. Bemis and Polly and the *Welweyas*, Pete and Shepp, spent many a Sunday evening watching the sun go down in the west as they listened to Viktor tell his tales.

Sometimes the *Welweyas* would try to follow Viktor on his excursions through the wilderness. As soon as they entered the forest they would lose him. One moment he would be there, the next he was gone, vanished. Tall and powerful, he seemed incapable of awkward movement. Wherever he went his progress was soundless. His comings and goings were like magic to Pete and Shepp, but were extremely disturbing to those who had reason to fear him.

One day Many Wounds fell ill. Slowly over the months, respect had changed to affection between the two men, and sorrow once again overwhelmed Viktor when he realized there was nothing he could do for his mentor. He carried the old man to his tipi and tenderly covered him with blankets, then prepared a brew that would lesson his discomfort. Whatever Viktor had given him had a calming effect and the pain dissolved.

When nothing more could be done, Many Wounds said, "It is time for me to sing my death song. I wish to do so in The Place Where the Earth Still Laughs so that when my song is finished I may join with Those That Walk."

Viktor called the Chestnut and made the old *te-wat* comfortable on his broad back, and the horse followed Viktor up the narrow and winding path, behind the silvery waterfall and across the meadow. The journey took two days. At the top the mist was like giant girls in white dresses, flinging themselves over the crestline trail and into the valley on the other side. Their tiny procession walked into clouds and the sun became the moon.

Viktor laid Many Wounds carefully down at the roots of the giant tree between the two pools. As he did so, the mist dissolved, as if showing the way for the great *te-wat* into the next world.

Many Wounds briefly opened his eyes and said, "It is enough."

For a long moment Viktor stood motionless in the shadow of the giant tree, then quickly, silently, while the sun was setting one last time on his friend, he glided across the meadow and quietly away.

The Chestnut followed, and the raptor circled overhead.

CHAPTER EIGHT

THE HOUSE stood as always—as you had left it three days before. Yet it was transformed. You saw it with new eyes, the eyes of a dreamer. It was exposed, sinister, cancerous, with festering injuries in places you hadn't noticed. Menacing in a way you had sensed but never really seen.

You climbed the steps to the front door, taking your time, reluctant to enter. You stopped again to gaze at the leering façade. You saw it now with different eyes, the eyes of one who has had a veil removed.

At the moment Corey went out the door, the house seemed to take a breath, expand, and then contract around you—one alone without a light. You wandered around feeling at a loss. You had no desire to paint or sleep or eat. You went upstairs, then back down again, aimlessly. You missed Corey.

It was hot for mid-October. But suddenly you were very cold, and went to put on a sweater. An icy wind seemed to blaze up in you as Corey drove away, with full fury now, causing a curious shrinking of your skin until you felt diminished, and the surface of your body was glowing blue with cold.

The rutted road home had wearied your legs and endless images of Those That Walk filled your head. Your nerves were stretched taut. The images forced their own solitude, coming and going, suddenly present for no reason, or no reason that made normal sense, and then they were gone again. You had the feeling that you were under water. You felt strangely discontent and a suffocating anxiety quickened your pulse.

You started for your studio in the cellar. As you stepped onto the basement stairs you were hit by a blast of cold, damp air. Out of nowhere came the sound of disembodied laughter and the cold intensified. The cold seemed a solid wall you had to push away in order to pass.

You stepped down and there at the bottom of the steps, crouched over a small brass box filled with keys, was a lean, big-boned man with a gray complexion. His skin in the occluding light of the cellar brought to mind dug-up slime. He had bird-darting cold eyes. He was a kind of carrion bird, a bone picker with no color—not in his face, his hair, his eyes, or his clothes. He looked up from the box of keys with the face of a carnivore.

Out of the shadows a huge, vulgar-bodied insect, seeking light, crawled from under the house and dropped on your bare neck. You shuddered and quickly brushed it away. When you turned back the Gray Man was gone.

Then, from nowhere, a long deep sigh filled the air, followed by heartbreaking weeping.

What was happening?

Your painting of the running woman hung, desperate, on the cellar wall. You turned to scramble back upstairs and the terribly mutilated figure of the woman from your painting came walking down the stairs toward you on legs hanging crookedly at an impossible angle. Her body was twisted at the waist and her head hung forward, disconnected, to the middle of her chest. The head lifted, independent of the torso, and her eyes were watching you— beseeching human eyes, looking straight at you.

You stood frozen to the spot, hypnotized by every detail of the horrible apparition.

There was a pathetic longing in her eyes. Unlike the Gray Man there was no harmful intention in her face. Out of doors, Freckles began howling, and as quickly as she appeared the woman vanished.

Frightened, you went to your room upstairs to watch for Corey's return. You lay down on your bed and closed your eyes. The air in the room shifted and your eyes flew open again to see the woman kneeling now at the foot of the bed. At the same instant you felt an evil presence move into place behind you at the head of the bed. Too frightened to turn and look, just as afraid not to, you went rigid with terror, knowing it was the Gray Man, Greegar's hump-backed specter.

Then the most terrifying thing. Perfectly felt, but not seen, the awful creature began to lower himself onto you, until you were pinned, helpless, suffocating to the bed. You were fully awake. You knew you were. In vain, you struggled to cry out. One scream and you would be free. You knew it. But you couldn't make a sound. Frantic, terrified, with all your might you fought to escape from beneath his cerement-like presence. You struggled in vain.

There was no release and your desperate cries found no voice. His dark, aborting hand round your throat smothered such cries. Madness lay there in the screams that were shattering against the walls of your skull, unable to escape. It felt as though a heavy plastic covering had been thrown over you through which no air could penetrate. With a superhuman effort you tried to sit up again. This time your violent struggle brought tears of relief when you plainly felt his weight rippling away.

Between blinks, seen but not seeing, you watched the gray apparition pass beside the bed from one corner of the room to the next. He wore a gray hat turned down at the brim. It covered his eyes, which somehow made him even more frightening. The sound of a woman crying in the darkness came again. Then a deep voice spoke to her sharply and she fell silent.

A black mist began to form now, spreading over the bed like the unfolding wings of a giant bird. As you stared, it pulled itself up and became a tall dark form. It appeared hooded and at first had no face. Then it turned its loathsome self toward you and you recognized the figure from the cellar. It was the Gray Man, the Ghost that had accompanied Greegar the night of the full moon, the dark one who came smiling into your nightmares.

The weeping woman reappeared with bowed head. She stood facing the wall. You sat up. She distinctly jumped and looked with fear on her face toward the door. The Gray Man had moved to stand across from her. They started to argue violently.

You sat on the edge of your bed watching, mesmerized. There was a sharp sound like glass shattering. The woman's hands flew up to the back of her head and she stumbled a few steps forward to fall on the floor in front of you. Her eyes rolled back as if she had just been hit on the back of the head. A trickle of blood started to ooze down over her forehead. Her eyes closed and you felt a terrific blow to the back of your own head and you were slammed off the bed and onto the floor.

Stupefied, you raised your head as an invisible force begin to dismember the fallen woman, ripping her apart at the joints. The Gray Man watched with you, grinning.

Two small hands took yours and tried to bring you to your feet. Then the tiny hands were pulling at your pant leg, trying to get your attention. The door knob to your room turned slowly.

You heard a cradle rocking and sad weeping; first the woman and then a child, then whispers in rhythm with the rocking cradle saying, "Don't open it. Don't open it."

Dust came up from the cellar through the vent. The bone-picking Gray Man spoke, *without speaking,* as he had before in the dream, "The child is my nephew. The child is my son. I buried it in the cellar when it couldn't hold up its deformed head any longer."

His breathing, deep and slow, came and went with the rocking of a toddler he held in his lap. Its big head was propped against his colorless chest. He sat for the longest time caressing the baby and looking at you—a recurring nightmare.

Still smiling, he took out a razor and drew it across the child's throat. It was the same razor he had put in Greegar's hand before. Blood poured into his lap, pooling on the floor.

You didn't hear much after that or see much either. Maybe because you were sitting in darkness looking into the remnants of the ghostly light for so long you were finding it harder and harder to focus your eyes. Tiny pinpoints of illumination drifted across your field of vision. You tried to blink them away. Then the flecks of light began to gather again and the nightmare repeated itself.

The woman wept. The Gray Man shouted her into silence. She fell, struck from behind and you felt the blow again on the back of your own head. The Gray Man sat on the window sill, rocking the deformed child and smiling malevolently. When he was sure you were watching, he took out his razor once more and slowly drew it across the throat of the sleeping child. Blood spilled over them both and onto the floor. You watched in horror as the Gray Man bent to drink from the child's open throat.

You could not think or see or hear anything, except that which was shown in this daytime nightmare. You stumbled to your feet, as the nightmare began to repeat for a third time. The house was a floundering ship sinking into a black hole, a gaping maw, sucking you toward deep waters and wreckage, filled with submerged secrets manifest in soggy, waterlogged corpses with leering eyes.

You rushed downstairs and outside without thinking, taking no particular path—just going where your blind and dumb body led you.

Shaped by the prospect of your imagination your divination on the mountain had become the blueprint of that day's events.

❀

Corey, meanwhile, was pulling up in front of Greegar's

rundown trailer on the outskirts of town. A glow of contentment from the three days out of doors with Clinton went with him. He felt immortal, like a god who could point to a bush and it would burst into flames. Greegar couldn't trouble him, he thought. By going to find out what Greegar wanted, he reasoned, he would be able to keep him away from Clinton. Clinton, with his doe-like skin and slender body covered with freckles. His trusting looks. His friend. The unfamiliar contentment frightened and pleased Corey. Since John had left it was the first time he'd wanted to be with anyone. It didn't occur to him to question what he was feeling. He was happy.

When the trailer came into view his contentment began to dissolve. He felt a pain and winced. The closer he came to home, if it could be called home, the more violent the pain, an agony so ferocious it seemed his bones were being scalded and he nearly turned back. He didn't need this. It wasn't really worth it, but he continued on anyway. Greegar's violence had begun to be directed toward Corey once John was gone, beginning in earnest the day Corey told Greegar that John had left and joined the Army.

At the news Greegar had lashed out and struck Corey several times across the face. His huge paw knocked Corey to the ground by the third blow.

Corey hardly made a sound. Only a small whimper escaped from between his clenched teeth. He had expected such a reaction. He'd helped John plan his escape. As they made their plans, they both knew Corey would become the brunt of Greegar's rage. They'd taken delight in planning little torments for Greegar and took the utmost pains to avoid being caught and blamed. A broken step. A missing distributor cap. Piss in his underwear drawer they'd blamed on a stray cat.

"No whimpering?" Greegar said that day as he systematically struck Corey up and down the back of his legs and across his shoulders. "You're more of a man than I thought!"

Abuse is a black art that calls for a perfect teacher. In blood and beatings, Greegar had carved his name on John, and then Corey, making stone boys of them. There is something not human about such a man who is able to stare unrepentant into the face of God while destroying innocence. In his instinct for self-preservation, Corey remained silent, knowing anything he said would only infuriate Greegar further.

"Must be you're ready for a grownup's responsibilities. Time to show a little gratitude to your old man for all he's done for you."

The fury in Greegar's voice shifted to something more sinister, and Corey knew what was coming next.

"Clever boy, I'm sure you'll take to it better than John. Even though you're getting a later start. Later-starters are always hungrier. And I like 'em hungry!"

Perhaps, if John had not run away, Corey would have been safe for a few more years. He was not innocent. How could he be, knowing what Greegar did to John so many nights? But part of him had managed to deny what his father was doing, even when he heard John's screams and saw the burns on his arms when he returned to their room at night. He had managed somehow to overlook the split lips and John's face covered with bruises.

It wasn't the beatings that Corey feared. It was the rest, which came swiftly on like a breath of foul air. Once Greegar knew that John was gone for good, Corey spent his sleepless nights covered in sweat and stinking of fear, waiting. He didn't wait long. It was his third sleepless night and just before dawn when Greegar strode into his room like the beast of prey that he was and tore the covers off, then paused for a moment in anticipation.

Corey, frozen, willed himself invisible. Leisurely, Greegar took hold of his son's T-shirt and jerked him up out of bed. Corey's neck snapped back and he went limp. Powerless, he hadn't the courage to resist. It was his father.

Next, Greegar put one hot hand inside Corey's undershorts and the look of lust on his face changed to one of surprise.

"Well, you certainly got more than your share. How nice for you. How nice for me. How nice for everyone."

He slid his vile hands up under Corey's shirt and laughed when Corey recoiled from his cold touch. He pushed the boy down onto the bed and discarded the remainder of his grubby clothes. He took hold of the belt from his abandoned pants.

Greegar's face told Corey this was to be no ordinary beating and something snapped in him. He began to struggle with a savage desperation, but quickly saw it was useless. Even if he had the strength, he didn't have the will. There would be no escape. In that moment of realization, he fell absolutely still. Hidden beneath this stillness was a fury so great at his helplessness that his mind left his body and watched detached as his father abused him.

The beatings were really the second step in Jack Greegar's demonic process. For years, as long as the boy could remember, there had been vague humiliations and endless curses directed at him, denigrating insults and a stinging slap now and then. When John left, the beatings quickly became regular and were ritualized by Greegar always announcing:

"It's time for your next lesson."

When the boy was nearly senseless and it was clear he could bear no more, Greegar would touch him, pressing the bruised places viciously and twisting his son's abundant genitals with a strange beatific smile on his face all the while.

The touching was the worst because, in the act, Greegar gave smutty names to Corey and what he was making him do. As if Corey and not Greegar were really to blame for what was happening. Of course, Greegar was really naming himself.

When Greegar tried to penetrate Corey the first time Corey silently vowed revenge. His desire for revenge became an ugly thing that fed on itself and grew.

"It's time for your next lesson."

Greegar was a complacent man and assumed his control over Corey was absolute. But Corey had determined in watching Greegar's systematic destruction of John that the same final humiliation would never happen to him. A part of him stayed removed from the degradation, stayed apart and waited for the right moment.

One night, when Greegar came crapulous into his room with rape in mind, Corey feigned compliance then, when Greegar turned away for a moment to kick off his boots, Corey drew back and with all his night delivered a blow to the side of Greegar's drunken head.

Greegar's eyes flew open in incredulous disbelief and Corey followed up with a swift elbow to his ribs. All his pent-up rage and humiliation were behind the blow. The air fled Greegar's lungs with a gasp and he clutched helplessly at his stomach, unable to breath. He grabbed at Corey but could not hold him. Corey struck again, this time a knee to the face.

"Never again will you touch me. Never—"

Corey stood for a moment watching his father gasping on the floor and then walked out. In that moment he became a man. He felt no remorse. Only a kind of ecstasy. He was free of Greegar's control, damaged, maybe irreparably, but free. A euphoric elation consumed him as he walked away. That day he moved into the loft in the barn at your mother's suggestion.

These recollections coursed through Corey as he wove through the familiar trailer park and pulled up in front of his old home. Greegar was waiting on the doorstep of his trailer, waiting with the singleminded ferocity that belongs only to the mad. At the sight of his father a flame of icy air exploded inside Corey's damaged heart and spread waves of disquiet surging through his chest. He gripped the steering wheel. He took a breath. The seizure whipped through him and was gone as quickly as it had come.

Greegar had spent the day working on a bottle of whiskey. He tossed off the last of it just as Corey stopped the truck. Greegar pushed himself to his feet. He swayed a little, but recovered, and made his way down the rickety steps. Inside the lanky, big-boned man, a sleeping serpent woke, instantly furious and ready to strike.

Corey got out of the truck.

Greegar watched him, calculating. He lit a cigarette and waited until the boy stood in front of him before he spoke.

"I need a new septic tank dug."

"So?"

"You're gonna dig it."

"What's the matter? You're so full of shit you don't know what to do with it all?"

"Careful what you say, punk. You're gonna do some work for your old man now, whether you like it or not."

"Now?"

"Ya, now. Where you been anyway? I been lookin' for you for three days."

"Up in the hills."

"With you little friend?" he sneered.

"That's right, with my friend." Quietly, surprising himself with the truth.

"If you intend to stay away from here, then I want half your wages."

"I told them I would work for room and board, so I wouldn't have to be around you anymore. I ain't got no wages to give you."

"Bullshit! Well, you better get some or you're gonna be right back where you belong. With me."

"We'll see about that."

"That we will. Just remember, you're still a minor and you'll work where I want, when I want, or I'll know the reason why." Greegar tossed his cigarette butt away. "Now git out back and get started."

"Or else what?"

"Or else you and I are gonna have a little conversation with the sheriff. And he can explain to you what you don't seem to understand."

"And what's that?"

"Where your responsibilities lie. And if that don't make it clear enough, then maybe Clint's mom and dad will be interested in knowing what you and he have been playin' with each other."

"You don't know shit about me and Clinton. So keep your foul thoughts to yourself."

Why are the wicked so strong? Why do they have such power over us? Why does goodness seem so unequal to the task of replacing damage done? In the face of everything there was a part of Corey that wanted to love his father, but he had never been given the chance or a reason. Greegar had provided food and a kind of shelter for Corey as a boy. He knew nothing better. So, like a stray animal that will stay with a cruel master, Corey for many years had tried to obey and even love Greegar. His father's cruel stewardship had defined the boundaries of his world. He knew nothing else, so he had tried to obey. Like any child, he needed to belong. But now he'd felt something more, something better, and Greegar sensed he was losing control over Corey. It maddened him.

Could true friendship make up for this lack of love, fill the gap, replace the emptiness, heal the wounds? Facing Greegar now, a great weight that had briefly lifted settled down over Corey's new self and his new feelings.

Maybe there will always be a struggle between fathers and sons, a drama that must be acted out in endless ritual, between helpless beasts in rut. Maybe Oedipus slew Laius not so much to pass, but to find his way. Maybe we are only creatures in caves who know no better, stinging, struggling scorpions fighting for the right to love, for control of our own destiny, or just to be free.

Corey's trip toward Greegar had begun with anxiety and moved into pain, the pain of memories. Memories like wicked dragonflies darting across the surface of a fetid pond. They conjured up images vivid and sharp, a quagmire of violent feelings Corey did not want to look at. Until now, with Greegar before him once more, the pain was near the boiling point, a sudden torrential scalding of tissue and bone, baring hurt feelings and lost capacities.

As Corey stared at his father, he realized that nothing was left but a metallic taste in the roof of his mouth. It was the flavor not of fear, but fury. This clarifying rage urged him to turn and leave, to get out, to shake himself free, once and for all, of his father's control. Somewhere, deep down, he knew that if he did not, he would never enter unencumbered the crossroads he'd come upon with Clinton. Maybe this was why he'd come home. Facing Greegar, he faced himself. It was perhaps the only way to act out the truth of what Clinton had seen in his divination.

With a flash Corey understood what Clinton had not. The divination on the mountain had been a message for Corey. He must pluck the rod from his own chest and place it at the feet of his oppressor and demand an explanation. And if no explanation, then an end. Would it be sufficient?

Would his father take up the rod and attempt to strike him down again? Greegar was easily the most evil man Corey had ever known. Had Clinton's friendship made him strong enough to now resist such a force?

"Dig your own shit hole and do your worst. I have better things to do." Corey turned to walk away. But Greegar had another card up his sleeve.

"Not so fast." He smiled gleefully. "It just so happens I got some letters here for you from John."

Corey stopped short.

"You want 'em . . . ? Dig the hole."

Reluctantly Corey turned back, like a wild animal whose every instinct warned him to stay away, but he was trapped and Greegar knew it.

"The shovel's out back. Dig a nice one."

Greegar laughed, turned on his heel, and re-entered the trailer.

Corey hesitated for a moment then reluctantly went to the back of the run-down trailer and started to work.

Inside, Greegar kept an eye on Corey through the window. Once he could see Corey was doing as he had demanded, he decided to wash up. The trailer smelled like rot and cigarettes. In the corners of the bathroom, which hadn't been cleaned in years, there were smears of mold beginning to climb the walls. He didn't even notice as he showered. He got back into his discarded clothes and moved across the grimy carpet, out the front door, and into the back where Corey was working.

He lit another cigarette.

Corey ignored him, working with a fury, to get done and get away. The hole was already four feet deep. Greegar watched for a while, silently, a nasty grin on his face, and then went back inside.

This routine went on for the rest of the afternoon, with Greegar periodically coming outside and smoking one cigarette after another as he watched Corey. By late afternoon the hole was nearly finished. Corey had been working without a break for three hours. He was covered with sweat and dirt and he was beginning to feel fatigued. Greegar's constant scrutiny was rubbing salt in a sore. But he refused to let Greegar get to him. Finally he leaned on the shovel and turned to his father.

"There. Satisfied?"

"I can't say that I am." He took a deep drag off his cigarette. "I'm afraid you put the dirt on the wrong side of the hole."

"What the fuck?"

"Just what I said. The dirt is on the wrong side. You're gonna have to start over."

Corey threw the shovel down in disgust. "You're really pushing it."

"That's too bad ain't it. You want the letters? Do it again."

Corey climbed out of the hole brushing off his levis. "You want another hole dug today, do it yourself. Otherwise I'll be back tomorrow. I have the milking to do over at Clinton's place. I'm through here."

"Very well, but if you want to hear from John again not only will you finish this hole and any other work I can think of, but you'll be livin' here again where you belong."

With a supreme effort of will Corey controlled his rage and moved over to climb up into the pickup. "I'll finish your goddamn hole, but if you think I'm gonna live here again you've got another think comin'."

Corey drove off with Greegar's shouts following him.

Back home, you had started the milking. Corey parked the truck and joined you in the barn.

"Thanks, Clinton. Sorry I took so long." He dumped oats in an empty stall and led in another milk cow.

"No problem. I couldn't stay in the house alone any longer." Then shaking with the memories of your grisly chimeras, "It's not the same when you're not around, Corey. I saw horrible things. Horrible. The *te-wat* was right. Two together with a light are strong. One alone takes his chances. Something terrible happened in this house. Something that is being acted out over and over again. I'm frightened. I hate to admit it, but I am. I feel weak and frail and small. I am ashamed."

Corey reached toward you and slipped his sheltering arm around your shoulder. You lowered your head and his cheek rested lightly on your hair. His embrace was a sanctuary, a safe-haven and seemed to say, "I have enough strength for both of us. Take some of mine."

While you were finishing the milking, your mom and

Jerry returned. Shortly after, Mom called out for you to come in and eat.

You did your best with dinner that night. But couldn't get much of it down. Talking was even more difficult.

Seeing with clearer eyes was not easy. Not knowing had been simpler. Separated from Corey, it seemed that you had lost your courage.

"Two with a light can come to no harm. If they match their strides and whistle."

All through dinner you wanted to get up and find a sheet of paper and draw your latest dream and thereby execute some kind of catharsis. Or just move over and stand near Corey, or hug your mother or Jerry and never let go. But instead you stared blankly at your untouched food, the red table top, their faces, and even when you heard footsteps upstairs that no one else seemed to hear and a jolt of terror returned, you did not move.

After dinner you and Corey took turns bathing and then went out to the loft in the barn and talked of nothing. Your paleness and his unspoken fury toward Greegar said it all.

You drew for an hour or so, Corey nearby, his shock of golden brown hair, still damp from his bath was caught like an angel's wing in the lantern light.

Drawing him had a calming effect and was something you loved to do. Each stroke of the pencil was a caress and it pleased Corey as well, although he never could have said so.

But then just as your dreads were beginning to fade a little, you saw something snap in Corey's face. You dropped the sketchbook as Corey clenched his fists, breathing fast.

"Are you okay, Corey?" You watched him struggling for air. "You didn't tell me what happened with Greegar. Are you okay?"

"Ya sure. No problem." He smiled a little trying to prove it.

But you sensed something more, something underlined by his clenched fists and the bunched muscles in his jaw. Some secret whose shape you only had to look to see. Silence can be the most eloquent indication of pain. You reached your fingertips toward his face to soften whatever it was away, searching for some further sign of what was so troubling.

Corey bore the burden of being a strong man with no words—strong arm, strong will, and strong desires, but few words to speak of them.

"My friend," you said, simply, still searching his face.

He blinked rapidly, as if there was something painful in his eyes. He rubbed them and ran his fingers back through his hair.

"Greegar has been getting letters from John. Letters for me. And he won't let me have them unless I move back home."

"That bastard!"

"You got that right."

"What are you going to do?"

"I don't know," he said. "I have to finish digging his septic tank. Maybe if I pretend to do what he wants he'll relent and give them to me . . . Then again, maybe not. I can take care of Greegar. More important, what are we going to do about your nightmares? Or whatever they are."

"I've been thinking about that. We should talk to the Vinegar Man. He'll know what to do. He helped before. Somehow I feel the Gray Man and Greegar are connected. By their evil intentions, if nothing more."

"You might be right Clint," said Corey. "I think it's a good idea to see what the Vinegar Man thinks. Tomorrow we'll go out to Rivertown and see what he has to say."

"I'm going to go get my sleeping bag. I'll be right back."

"I'll be here."

You scrambled down the ladder from the loft and hurried into the house. "Mom!" you called. "Where are you?"

"Upstairs, Clinton."

You hollered up the stairs. "Is it okay with you if I stay out in the loft with Corey tonight? We want to go over to Rivertown first thing in the morning."

"That's fine with me," she said. "Just make sure you finish your chores before you take off. Dad will be back this weekend and we want everything to be in order for his return. Okay?"

"Okay, Mom."

You wanted to get another sketchbook. The one you had been using was nearly full and all your materials were in the cellar studio. You took a breath and plunged down the stairs. There was nothing there out of the ordinary. It made no sense. Maybe the specters only appeared when you were alone, as the *te-wat* had warned.

Then, from out of the darkness, a voice whispered in your inner ear. "Don't leave me." It froze the blood in your veins.

It was the woman from your vision who had manifest herself in your painting.

You answered her plea silently. "I'll be back."

You grabbed a sketchbook and dashed up the stairs to the porch where you picked up your sleeping bag and headed toward the barn.

The desperate voice of the woman rang in your head.

"Don't leave me! Don't leave me!"

What did she want? What could you do? The Vinegar Man would know. It was with this thought in mind that you crawled into your sleeping bag next to Corey in the loft and fell asleep.

CHAPTER NINE

FTER COREY left, Greegar continued his drinking and went to bed thoroughly intoxicated. He woke late the next afternoon to obsessive thoughts about Corey and Clinton. He'd been having such thoughts for days now. There had been such an overwhelming sense of satisfaction watching Corey working in his back yard, at having the boy in his control again. He grinned as he remembered telling Corey the dirt was on the wrong side of the hole, cackling out loud at his own cleverness. His laughter brought on a painful ringing sound in his inner ear and his mood quickly shifted. The noise had been coming and going for the last several weeks. It was a kind of ringing, some great bell tolling, calling him, that resounded throughout his whole being.

It always started with heat in his loins and he felt pleasure, but as it continued unabated, it was maddening and drove him, goading him forward to he knew not what.

Today the ringing gave way to a sonorous ticking at the base of his spine, a resounding, even-paced, pendular sound, steadily increasing in tempo and volume until his brain pounded with it. At its highest pitch, when he was certain he could bear no more, the awful noise blossomed into a maelstrom of demon voices.

He staggered outside. The impact of the voices overpowered him and he sagged down on the front steps. For an instant they stopped. In the resounding silence he felt an urgent need to rush forward. He scrambled to his feet only to be blinded by the returning maelstrom. His hands flew to his ears. He groaned and dropped to his knees. Whole symphonies of sound plucked the synapses in his brain, like tortured violins, discordant, painful, urgent. He took a shuddering breath.

Without lessening, the voices slowly integrated with his subconscious and became bearable. Only then was he able to stand and move to his truck. He leaned there for a moment, further collecting his strength before climbing inside.

He managed to light and inhale deeply on a cigarette. The voices shifted, becoming some wild, mythic beast screaming at the core of him. He could actually see the animal sitting on the dashboard of his truck. It was a deformed monster, with talon-like hands, bloody teeth, and a twisted back. It smiled at him! A friend, its bloody mouth opened and the shrieking became a command.

"Take Mary. She is waiting. She is yours. I give her to you."

The ghoul thinned out for a moment, then clotted like

191

blood, shrieking its desires, which were Greegar's desires, his body a cold cavern where the beast nested. It clawed at his entrails, feeding, tearing bits of flesh from his lungs and heart and liver as it howled its wishes.

"Corey must not escape. He is yours. Your plaything. Take him. Take Mary. Ruin Clinton."

Greegar started the truck and headed toward the setting sun, toward Rivertown.

🐚

After chores the next afternoon, you and Corey walked down the embankment from the house and toward the river road hoping to find the Vinegar Man. It was a perfect autumn afternoon. You cut through the ragged woods passing a place you knew where wild roses grew.

"How about if we take some roses to Mary?" said Corey.

A curious confusion of emotions washed over you, but you responded steadily, "Sure, why not?"

As had become your custom, Corey went first, stepping lightly, swerving to avoid boughs, looking straight ahead, leading the way. Freckles, who had come along, suddenly darted forward and stopped in a stiff point. He had scented something unusual. Corey looked inquiringly at the dog, then glanced around to you. Lifting his feet lightly and straining his eyes before him, Corey passed carefully through a thicket of roses, and came in line with the dog's point. For one second Corey stood as rigid as Freckles. You closed in behind.

There, trapped in a bog, was a yearling mule deer. It began to struggle frantically when it scented the dog, miring itself further in the soggy ground.

You helped Corey drag a log over and drop it across the bog in front of the struggling animal. Freckles set to barking furiously, further terrifying the poor beast.

"Freckles, be still! Sit!" commanded Corey.

Corey did a balancing act down the length of the log toward the deer.

"Steady there, fella. We don't want to hurt you."

It tossed its head, eyes rolling wide with fear.

"Steady, steady. It's okay."

He'd come even with the animal and crouched down, still talking quietly, reassuringly.

"We're gonna help you. But you have to be still. Okay?"

From his point of leverage on the log, Corey slowly and gently reached forward to take hold of the yearling's budding antlers. It went wild. Corey held on for dear life while the yearling bucked and tossed his head. Then one of its hooves came free and was planted on the log. Corey put all his weight and strength into pulling the animal forward as it dug at the log with its freed front hoof. With a sucking sound, slowly, reluctantly, the earth gave up its prey and Corey let loose, falling backward off the log as the animal scrambled its way out of the swamp. It paused for a moment on dry ground, tossed its head and shook itself, then disappeared into the trees.

You let loose a triumphant whooping and Corey grinned happily.

"Are you okay?" you asked, seeing Corey scratched and muddy, still clinging to the log.

"Sure I'm okay. It's free isn't it?"

"Yes, it's free."

"Now how about those roses?" and he scrambled to his feet.

The sun was just setting.

❧

At Rivertown, it seemed as if the Vinegar Man had been waiting for us. You described your Vision Quest to him and he listened carefully without interrupting. Corey handed his handful of wild roses to Mary during the telling. She smiled her thanks. When you described Those That Walk, and the ritual dance of Many Wounds, the Vinegar Man nodded his head in acknowledgment.

"What does it all mean?" you said as you finished.

"Who are the dark ones that tried to pull Clinton through the falls?" added Corey.

"What is the connection between the Gray Ghost from the house and Greegar?"

"First things first, boys," and the Vinegar Man paused, contemplating. "Clinton has become a Dreamer. That much is clear. And Corey, you are a protector, a brave. One of those honorable men of action who facilitates the visions of their *te-wat*s. Sometimes it is done willingly, sometimes without the warrior knowing he is fulfilling prophecy."

He went on. "A Dreamer's vision may have a personal message for the one who receives it or the dream may speak to the whole tribe. But here is the difficult part and the real test. Such dreams can be symbols or abstractions of desires, if you will. Sometimes they are metaphors for what may happen or what should happen."

194

"I'm sorry, but I'm confused," said Corey honestly.

"I have to admit I am, too. A little," you added.

"The point is this," the Vinegar Man explained. "You must divine the message of the vision for yourself for it to have any meaning or power."

You looked disappointed, so he went on. "Besides I think you already know what much of what your experience means. Some of it doesn't need to be spoken aloud, I think. Some of it does." He scratched among his whiskers. "There is one way I can help."

"How is that?" you asked in chorus.

"On your quest, Hunyahwat gave you your Dreamer names. They will give you strength to see and follow the truth."

"He did?" asked Corey.

"Yes, for certain he did," the Vinegar Man returned.

"What are they?" you asked, mystified, but the Vinegar Man was not to be hurried.

"The one who initiates the pilgrimage, the one who points the way, has the right and the responsibility of identifying the Dreamer names given during the quest."

"That was you."

"Yes, that was me. And now I need a moment to be certain that I have correctly determined your eponyms."

Having thus spoken the Wizard of Dreams ceremoniously removed a pinch of herbs from the pouch at his waist. He sifted the pungent leaves from hand to hand for a moment. First with his right and then with his left, he sprinkled the leaves on the fire. The flames blazed up incandescent in a multitude of giddy colors. With what seemed to take supernatural effort, he raised his left hand

and placed it behind the head of Corey. His right, he placed behind yours. Sparks from the fire glittered there, in his open hands, creating a nimbus around your heads. A strange aroma filled the air and the wizard spoke as if with the voice of Hunyahwat.

"Stands Like Elk," he intoned toward Corey, and then, "Falls Through Water," toward you.

"Stands Like Elk."

"Falls Through Water," you repeated respectively.

The Vinegar Man explained further. "An Elk fights for the right to lead, and then defends the herd with his life. This is a very powerful name and was given to you by the fox at the edge of the meadow. Clinton, you have been honored greatly, you were given your agnomen by Those That Walk, while 'Between' and under protest from the powers of darkness."

The Vinegar Man leaned back. His ritual had exhausted him—no shaman now, just a tired old man.

You shivered at his words. "And this makes me the personal enemy of the Gray Man who is one of them."

"Yes, he is one of the dark ones, like those who pulled you through the falls. You begin to understand."

"And Greegar?" asked Corey.

You answered, "Greegar is the Gray Man's twin in this world," and then with a premonition, you spoke again, as one who sees: "He is coming here—now."

"Well, Stands Like Elk isn't ready to see him again just yet. So I suggest we fade away." Corey, the cautious warrior that he was, had spoken.

The Vinegar man nodded agreement, vaguely. The effort it had taken him to name your Dreamer names had obviously exhausted the old visionary. He was falling asleep.

Corey whispered, "Let's watch from the woods and see if Greegar really is coming."

"All right," you returned. "It doesn't look like the Vinegar Man can help us any more tonight."

You slipped into the friendly darkness of the woods. The Vinegar man began to snore.

Rivertown waited.

Greegar parked his truck at the river road bridge to avoid detection, hoping to catch Mary alone or give himself some other predatory advantage. Cloaked by darkness, he arrived at the camp undetected, a shadow hunchbacked by a ghost.

Simultaneously, you and Corey circled away, a perfect counterpoint to Greegar's stealthy approach.

Two of Rivertown's more regular inhabitants, Joe and Mannie, were playing cards by lantern light. Joe was a drunk and Mannie, good-natured and not too bright, was his favorite opponent. Joe liked playing with Mannie because the poor dumb-bunny never got mad when he lost or was cheated. Mary watched, seated on the stoop of the Vinegar Man's shack. The Vinegar Man nodded and snored at her side.

Greegar, guided by his voices, paused in the shadows at the edge of the woods. Joe glanced up, stared into the darkness for a moment, and then spit.

"Did you bring any whiskey?"

Greegar moved out from the darkness near Mary. She shifted weight, chilled. Mannie shuffled cards at the makeshift table.

Mary covered her arms and leaned away from Greegar, "Can I deal the cards this time Mannie?"

"Hell, I just got 'em started."

"Come on Mannie," Mary coaxed.

"Ya, baby, come on. Deal the cards for us," Greegar said and stepped into the campfire light, bringing part of the night with him. Mannie and Joe moved aside to give Greegar room. He sat and pulled out his flask.

Mary shifted weight, pushed off the side of the shanty and walked over to take the cards. When Greegar was settled, Mary began to deal the cards from the opposite side of the table. The wind came up, sparking the fire, then stopped abruptly. A willow leaf spiraled out of the night sky.

Mary dealt the cards, counting carefully, placing Greegar's in the middle of the table where he had to reach for them.

"Oh, you do that so nice." Greegar licked his lips.

Joe flinched. Greegar held out his flask suggestively. Mary shook her head and dealt the cards.

"A drink or two, a drink or three, then you'll want to poke at me."

"That's right, Mary. That's right, girl." He slapped the table and snorted. "No one puts anything past Mary."

Mannie grinned and picked up his cards. The Vinegar Man slept, undisturbed. Joe spat again.

The game got started. Mary didn't play. She just dealt the cards. During the hands she moved away to stir a catfish stew bubbling on the fire. She would return to the table when it was time to deal again. Each time she came back, Greegar pushed the flask, which had gone around the table twice now, in her direction. The first few times she shook her head, but the third time she picked it up, turned her back to the table and took a drink.

It wasn't much of a game, which was fine with Greegar. He kept the bottle going around until Joe had slumped over the table unconscious. Shortly after, Mannie stumbled away to his bedroll. The Vinegar Man slept on, oblivious. Just as Greegar had hoped, he and Mary were left alone at the table. The only thing he hadn't figured on was you and Corey watching, hidden in the shadows. Silently, as his voices instructed, Greegar passed Mary the whiskey once again.

His face, like a carnival mask on a pole, hung and swayed over the makeshift table.

The Gray Man whispered inside his head, "It is time."

Without warning Greegar reached out and grabbed the front of Mary's dress, ripping it open to the waist. His gaping mouth swallowed the moon. A look of surprised confusion came over Mary's face and then she twisted away and tried to run, but he lunged after her and grabbed her again. This time the back of her dress. Her confusion turned to terror. With two quick, violent jerks, he ripped her dress the rest of the way off and spun her around to face him again, hungry to see her exposed breasts, full and tender. He closed one hand over her throat to prevent her from screaming. He looked to the Vinegar Man and then back to Joe, slumped over the table. Neither moved. So with his other hand he pawed and twisted and pinched her nipples, and then slowly began to draw her to him, a reptile preparing to devour its prey.

Viciously he knocked her feet out from under her and pushed her to the ground where he threw his full weight upon her nearly naked body. He clawed at the material still covering her hips and ran his dirty hands up between her legs. His body weight forced them apart. He ground his hips against hers, pressing his genitals against her soft flesh. He was not hard. Realizing this, he stood and jerked her up onto her knees and began to force her face toward his crotch.

"Suck it, bitch. You'll be glad you did when you see how big it gets!"

From the darkness outside the campfire light, you looked at Greegar, his back to you, and felt hate being born in a spasm of flesh and blood torn from the soul. It was blinding, like being forced to stare into a smoldering, black sun.

I turned and watched Corey watch Greegar and I hope I never again see the look I saw at that moment on Corey's stricken face.

Then, before you knew what he intended, Corey had moved quickly and quietly, to the back of the Vinegar Man's shack. Without a sound, he returned to the edge of the campfire light. He carried a shovel. Then, like an avenging angel, he stepped into the light with this spade, his rod and arrow raised high.

The shovel hit Greegar in the back of the head with a sickening thud and he slowly began to crumble to his knees and one hand, where he seemed to rest for a moment, until he slid face-first into the dust at Mary's feet.

There was no blood and for a moment you thought it hadn't happened. But it flashed past again; Corey taking the shovel and swinging it overhead from behind and it coming down hard, with a thud. And again you seemed to see him take it and swing it up wildly before bringing it smashing down on Greegar's bowed head, as he pressed Mary's face between his spread legs. And again, and again. As if somehow Corey was condemned to repeat the act endlessly. The arching path of the blow burned in the air, vibrated there, even as Greegar crumbled to lie in curious supplication before Mary, before us all.

Mary scrambled to her feet and tried to cover herself. The Vinegar Man and then Joe, started awake. Corey stood frozen. The earth seemed to shift in its path and hang motionless. In horror, Corey dropped the shovel, recoiling. He looked wildly right and left, and then his muscles contracted with a will of their own and he hurled himself into the darkness, running straight for the river.

Without thinking, you scrambled after him.

As you rushed away, Joe and Mannie and the Vinegar Man gathered around the fallen body wreathed by the campfire light. In the darkness, in the night, Greegar, like all men, lay equal.

Corey crashed away, a wounded deer pursued by wolves, under branches, over logs, sloshing and falling in ankle-deep bogs. Rushing out wildly, trying to fall away in the darkness from the terrible act left behind. You followed, swimming through willow trees that tried to strangle you, then out into chilling moonlight, and back again.

Dry stones warned of the upcoming river. They were leaden beasts smashed underfoot, marking your flight on into the river, knee deep and cold. Only then did Corey slow down.

He stood frozen, took a step, turned again, this time to

start up river, hesitated, then down. He took another step away and stopped, still standing midstream. His panting mingled with the sound of the water. Then began to soften and slow and faded into the rest of the night.

You waded in after him. "The Wagstaff's barn is just over there."

It was easy to find, looming through the trees. In the moonlight it cast a long shadow over an alfalfa field, curving up the hill behind. Mostly unused, the barn was completely open on one side and looked out onto the curving field. Inside you found discarded harness and broken bales of hay. As you entered, a barn owl swooped out and away like an omen. The breath from its wings feathered your face as it passed. The night had taken on a certain hush, a kind of wondering.

You found a horse blanket and old flour sacks and made a nest in the straw. You led Corey over and got him to sit down. For the longest time he just sat and stared out into the night. Finally, he started to rock and cry a little. His choking cries caught in his throat, anguished, lost, swelling into gut-wrenching sobs that broke your heart. He moved you like the evergreen-covered hills, but for the moment he didn't even seem to know you were there. Then he turned and looked at you and something in his face broke. He gasped for breath as if the air had been sucked out of the night and started to reach to you. He stopped short, trembling. He turned to stare back out into the field, hesitant, seeming to want to flee again, or scream, but he did nothing. Only his haunted eyes spoke. Then his choking sobs came again, tearing at your insides and he covered his face with his big hands.

There was a primitive, animal quality to his grief. Even

in this moment of terrible distress his features were Orionesque and princely, but his eyes were the soft startled eyes of a newly awakened, troubled child.

"It's not your fault. It's going to be okay, Corey."

Wrenched out, "Ya, sure. It's okay. That bastard!"

You couldn't stand it anymore so you moved over and put your arm around him to try to give comfort. What else could you offer?

"Ah, Clinton. What am I going to do?" Utterly lost. Then, "That bastard. How could he do that? She hated it, hated it."

He calmed a little, and began to rock himself again with your arm still around his shoulders.

"He made me hate. He was filled with hate. That was his gift to the world. To John, to Evaline, to me. To everyone he knew. To everyone he ever touched. He made me hate, too, but I still wanted it. Taking it when it's not given is stealin'. It's worse. It's stealing from God. I couldn't let him do it again." Then low and ashamed, before he hid his face in his hands, "I saw him and John. And I liked it, Clinton. Something in me liked it. He had me, too."

You cradled him and said, "No, Corey. That's not it. He didn't have you. He took you, but he didn't have you."

"For a second, when I hit him, I killed it. This desire I have in me. For a moment it was gone, my wanting what he wanted from Mary. It was gone."

"No, Corey. That's not it. That's not what you wanted." You took your arm away and turned in to him so you would watch his face. You didn't have the words.

Then simply, "I feel safe with you, Corey."

"I don't know why you should."

"You're not mean to me anymore."

203

"Right. I just smashed my dad's skull in, and you feel safe."

"That's different," you continued, searching for a way you both could understand. "Remember that night when you asked me if I wanted to touch you? You wanted to touch me, too. I know, Corey. It's okay. Why do you think I followed you through the cornfields all those times and brought you water, even before we were friends?" Then, searching for a way to try and tell him, "You're like the scent of new-mown hay to me."

Through the shock a light began to dawn for Corey.

"I don't know nothin'."

"That's not true, Corey. You know a lot. You've showed me a lot, you're the best. I know you think I'm the smart one. But you know lots of things I don't. I wish I could show you."

"Clinton, show me how not to be ashamed. Teach me what it is I really want." He spoke these words, earnestly, almost desperately, then lay back, still watching you.

How do you love when all you've been taught is brutality? You couldn't speak. You could only hug yourself a little, trying to slow the fast beating of your heart. Something in your body had loved Corey even before your conscious self. Your heart had known what your mind was slow to accept. And now your racing pulse was urging you to tell him what you had come to feel for him. It seemed that here, tonight, all things could be said in this place at the end of the world. Corey's act had begun a reordering. So you had to speak or lose your chance to make sense of your feelings. For hope to grow out of death, for love to grow out of an act of retribution, of vengeance, of hate.

He watched you silently as you moved over to him. For

a moment you were terrified. But when you climbed on top of him, and your body, slighter, fit perfectly into the outline of his, he sighed and some of his grief shuddered away. He took hold of you fiercely and buried your face in his neck.

"I don't know nothin'."

"Be still . . . sorry, my hand is cold."

"I'll warm it." Then, "It's my big dick isn't it?"

"It's everything. Be still now. Take rest now. Heaven blest now."

At some point he took off his clothes and then helped you with yours. He pulled you over on top of him again and your stiff little dick was lost in the folds of his big one. His musky smell and the hay enveloped you.

Not much else happened.

For a while, maybe, Corey forgot what we had left behind in Rivertown. Forgot Greegar grabbing at Mary and her frantic attempts to get away. Forgot the shovel arching through the air and Greegar face down in the dust. Forgot because you were trying to climb inside each other, wrapping yourself in each others arms, weaving desire into something more—a releasing of shame for Corey, a further bonding for you.

You touched him everywhere, laughing in admiration when he got hard, shivering when he put his hands on you. Making things okay. For a time, forgetting what might be coming next, and what had happened. Taking delight in discovering your body and his tender response to it. The night wind, the returning owl, the willow trees weeping on the river, joined us. The cavernous barn creaked and moaned sheltering our contentment, finding sanctuary in being known at last. Lost, but now found.

At certain junctures Corey paused and looked at you questioning, but each time continued when you said, "It's okay, Corey. It's okay."

And it was.

Finally, just before falling asleep, Corey whispered at the back of your neck, "You were right, Clinton. He never had me, not like this. He never had me at all."

Is this what happens to the little boys who have no one to teach them their prayers? Is it true the Sandman isn't able to lure them into their dreams, but comes martyred, shot in the back by their innocent neglect. But maybe, if they are lucky, God sends another boy instead, someone to watch while they sleep. Isn't this the way it is supposed to be? Winkin' and Blinkin' sailing off together. Watched over by willows and the wind sighing through the barn. It must be, because for a single night we did sail away together. On golden sails, sails of woven air, sails spread to catch the wind—owl's wings to carry us.

The next morning you woke to Corey watching your face. Your eyes met for a moment and then he asked, "Clinton?"

"Yes?"

"Who am I?"

You hesitated, wondering what he was feeling, and then simply said, "You're the best."

"And you? Who are you?"

"I'm next-to-the-best."

It must have been enough, because he said, "Always," and pressed your hand to his cheek.

They found us the next morning coming through the fields, up from the river. The sheriff was there and a second patrol car. The Vinegar Man was there, too.

Greegar was dead.

Your mom stood wiping her hands on her apron. Dad sat on the porch steps, pulling on his irrigation boots.

Mom came to meet us saying, "Ah, Corey." Then to herself as the sheriff took him by the shoulder, "Why is it the wicked have such power over us? The devil controlled the switch in that man's brain, and that's a fact. What has happened was an act of mercy."

They took Corey away in the patrol car. You shook hands, then held hands through the window. It was outwardly harder for you than him.

Seeing the look on your face, he said, "It's okay, Clinton. I'm free." And the image of the yearling escaping the swamp flashed past. "I'm okay. It's okay."

But it wasn't.

At the trial Viktor returned from inside the Vinegar Man's head to testify on Corey's behalf.

"I don't know about the lawfulness of what Corey did. But in the face of what is right and wrong, he did no evil. He saved Mary and maybe himself. If society handles it right, this boy may rid himself of his past. Break a pattern. He gave Mary back to me and his future back to himself."

He had mumbled and shuffled his way to the witness stand, but when he looked out at those gathered there his eyes were bright and clear. It was Viktor the mountain man who peered out from the Vinegar Man's King Lear exterior and it was Viktor who spoke in Corey's defense.

"Forget the law," he said. "Think of justice. And give this boy back his life. Show him how to begin again."

They charged Corey with manslaughter and sent him to reform school. There was no one to speak of it with. He was seventeen. I was fifteen. I missed Corey terribly and the mere mention of his name opened a deep wound in me. I lived in a house of sorrow. We had lost each other to the larceny of fate.

Summers, they released Corey to foster homes to work. I begged my father to let him come stay with us. But he would have none of it. On his way to Rivertown that last day, Greegar had spoken to your parents, imparting one last poisonous gift.

Later your father said to you, "The things you and Corey did together were wrong." His lips curled as he spoke, as if by saying it so he could end it.

I know now that my father feared delicacy as if it were a mortal sin. Then I only knew that for a moment I hated him for his contempt of me and I understood, at least in part, how Corey had felt about his father. I also knew why I'd come to love Corey. My father's words made it all come clear. Corey's strong, uncritical maleness had been a sanctuary where I was safe from my father's first silent, then spoken disdain.

Four years later, I heard they were releasing Corey. He was twenty-one. Rumor had it that they were setting him up with forestry work in southern Utah. Supposedly his probation officer owned some cabin sites and a saloon where Corey was to be given room and board in exchange for work.

After Greegar's death, the Ghost in the house had no power over me. It disappeared. I don't know why. Not long after Corey's trial we moved to a place across the valley. Over the years we watched one family after another move into the house and then out again. No one ever stayed more than a year. Finally it was sold, and the new owners remodeled from top to bottom. They, too, only lasted a year. The last time I was home it was empty again.

As a child I thought the man in the moon was a boy with a pail. I imagined him, night after night, filling his pail with moonlight and then spilling it out again. Today everyone yearns for magic, for truth, or love, or simply for someone to make sense of things. We keep looking for heroes, but somewhere along the way we forgot how to become heroes ourselves. How can we? We've gone to the moon yearning to help the boy fill his pail and he was not there to greet us. We've cut down the old forests and Those That Walk weep, unheard, into the wind.

In the past, with Corey, it was always summer, and for one brief moment I didn't need the Sandman to lure me into slumber.

Today, for me, the Sandman sleeps with the dead. No tricks, no magic, no bedtime stories. He sleeps the sleep of despair and I enter my dreams alone, unattended. But in my memories of the past, with Corey, the summer has no end.

Here and now I've come to wear my armor well. Helmet and gorget and brassard and gauntlet. First assembled with the help of my father, that silent man who was always present but never there, who told me what I felt for Corey was wrong. So now I wear my armor in fear.

Fear that if I'm vulnerable, if I let my true feelings show, I'll be cut by the enemies of my tenderness and bleed to death. So instead I slowly suffocate behind my chain mail, trying vainly to peer through my clamped shut visor to see who is standing across from me. It seems I must choose between bleeding to death or smothering.

Do we find happiness so seldom that when we come across it we crush it underfoot in our astonishment?

I remember my father asking me once why I didn't paint anymore. I was surprised he had to ask, surprised he asked at all.

I once saw a beautiful young woman following a handsome dark-haired man through a park. She was in a white dress with an umbrella. He wore a rumpled suit and was unshaved. Let the girl be a young man, following with a book. Is it really so different? My father thought so. And his condemnation colored everything that had happened between Corey and me.

EPILOGUE

WELL, COREY, I don't know if you'll get this or not. I might not send it. I don't really know where you are, but the last I heard you had located in Springdale, Utah, and that you would be working at a saloon called the Bit and Spur.

I also heard you were doing some work for the Forest Service. That would be good. I'm happy for you. I have to say that the possibility that you won't read this allows for a certain spontaneity.

Three years ago I moved to California to go to art school. I stopped painting for a long time and then one day just took it up again. My eye is still good but my hand has lost its technique.

The time we spent together on the river has come to seem like a dream. But then you know that my dreams always seemed to me to be more real than what was real. So it's okay.

I'm writing this while sitting on a bench in a Japanese

garden not far from where I live. Things are blooming, tall yellow iris, tulip trees, hibiscus that are yellow and red. In front of me lily pads lie sprawled on the surface of a pond, like a large woman for Gauguin in full skirts on the floor. Gauguin was a famous painter of dark-skinned Tahitian women. The lilies are the rubies and the sapphires in her clothes and in her hair. There are palm trees here, Corey, and birds of paradise and nightblooming jasmine. I'd never seen a real palm tree before I moved to California. It's very different from Idaho. I miss the smell of pines and cedar. And I miss watching the willows weep down by the river where we used to go.

So, you're living in Springdale. I got your address from my mom. I don't think I ever told you, but my family comes from southern Utah. My Grandpa David helped build the road through there. The one that goes through Zion National Park. He surveyed the route for the government and then started construction with a friend of his, whose name was Art DeMille. Art married grandpa's sister, my great aunt Thora.

Is this confusing?

I was thinking about all that this morning as I was sitting on my doorstep smoking a cigarette. My dad grew up there in Rockville, Utah. Right next to where you are going to be in Springdale.

Grandpa David and his wife, Rosalie, had nine kids. My dad is in there somewhere—third, I think. I have aunts and uncles, my dad's brother's and sisters, buried there. Art and Thora are buried there as well. Grandpa David, my father's father, is too. He was killed one day coming back from work in the canyon. His pickup truck went off the road. My dad was ten years old at the time.

While I was sitting on the step this morning, the little Mexican girl who lives in the back ran by smelling of soap. Her two little brothers followed. One, a toddler in diapers, was pushed along in front by the other hurrying to catch up.

We've lived in a half-dozen places since you were last home. Finally, Dad moved the family back to Warren my last year of high school. They've been there ever since. I went with them briefly, then came here to California and art school. This is my third year on my own. I feel like I don't belong. I'm homesick. I miss the mountains. I went back to Idaho last summer when my dad died. I don't know if you knew. Funerals are such a strange thing. I think the *te-wat*s had the right idea. Sing your own death song with those who are close to you and then walk off into the forest. I went to church. Remember church? Amazingly enough, a lot of the same people are still there, more like ghosts than people. Maybe I, too, am thinning out, disappearing. I didn't feel like I belonged there either anymore. I guess I'm homesick for something that doesn't exist.

I think my dad was always homesick for the days he spent, the childhood he spent, in southern Utah. He never said as much, but when his dad died, I have a feeling his childhood ended. His mother, Rosalie, my grandmother, was left with nine kids. There was Cecilia, Bud, Lawrence (my dad), Lillian, Grace, Dean, Beverly, and Robin. Stan, the youngest, had just been born.

At dad's funeral, his younger sister, my Aunt Lillian came reminiscing. Her kind wrinkled face was a record of her acquired sorrows as a farmer's wife and this latest grief.

"Did you know that your dad and I were close as kids?"

How they must have been as children! Seeing my father's face there in hers I could not speak for heartache.

"Yes, we were always close. It never bothered your dad to have his little sister tagging along. I remember when our pa died—your Grandpa David. We were so young. I chased your dad around that whole summer. No one knew what was going to happen now that Pa was dead. So no one kept much track of us kids."

She placed a weathered hand on my arm, thinking to distract me from my grief by speaking of her own father's passing.

"Your dad taught me how to sit on a horse that summer. He was only ten years old, but already he could ride a horse like a man. Mama had just had a new baby boy. During all the trouble, she wasn't able to take good care of him. So she gave Baby Stan to Thora and Art. They had no children. When it came time to leave Rockville, mama went to get the baby and it wouldn't stop crying."

I asked her, "Why?"

"Well, the baby didn't know its own mother anymore."

"How sad for Grandma Rosalie."

"That wasn't the worst. Cecilia, the oldest, had just turned sixteen. She started to gain weight and have pains in her stomach. So those busybody Mormon bitches began to gossip. Cecilia had just started her menses, so when they stopped, the gossips said she was pregnant."

"She wasn't?"

"Damn right she wasn't. She had appendicitis and it was diagnosed too late and so she died. I'll always blame those Mormon women for that."

I touched her papery hand where it rested on my arm. "What a terrible summer for grandma." Then almost to myself, "Her husband is killed in an accident, her newborn baby bonds to another woman, and her oldest daughter dies of appendicitis."

"It would have killed a weaker woman," Aunt Lillian insisted. "Yes, then she up and moves from southern Utah to central Idaho to marry a man she has only corresponded with. You won't remember Grandpa Tidwell."

"Only his name. And his son, Uncle Roy Lee."

"Yes, Roy Lee is built just like his daddy. Pa Tidwell must have weighed three hundred pounds. The Lord gave mama one more baby so Pa Tidwell could have a son and maybe to make up for the ones mama lost. My, he was a big man. He scared the beans out of me at first."

"What happened to the rest of you?"

"We got dragged along. All seven of us!" she smiled, wrinkling further, and remembered.

When Grandma Rosalie was an old, old woman, she stayed with our family for a while and I remember she would put the long-dead Cecilia to bed and then curl up to go to sleep on the floor where we would find her. She used to keep big white mints in her purse, my grandma, that we would suck on in church. I remember. She kept them wrapped in a lacy blue handkerchief.

Aunt Lillian went on to tell me that Rosalie gave Baby Stan to Thora and Art to keep when she left Rockville. I met Thora and Art and Uncle Stan when I was eleven. It was at the same house in Rockville where Grandma Rosalie had lived, where Cecilia had died, where Stan was born and raised—the house where Lillian and my dad played as children. In the backyard was a huge boulder, nearly as big as the house.

Great Aunt Thora, who was still living in the house then, told me, "It just rolled down the hill one day."

When we knew dad was going to die I passed through Rockville again on my way back to Idaho.

They say you're a virgin until someone close dies, then grief wells up from a bottomless pit and you sit like some great wounded beast, a stone, because you know now you will die too. I had fevers that whole trip, flashing hot and cold. I dreamed I cradled a sleeping baby in my nightshirt, a boy.

I held my dad and my mom in my arms that summer. One of two or three times in my whole life. I needed to touch him to believe he was going. I touched him again in the coffin, his hand, to know he was dead—to know in fact that this invincible force I'd known all my life had been reduced to a frail little body, shrouded in its burial garments, and that he was dead.

My father slept sitting up that summer, unable to breathe lying down. I slept on the ground near the boulder in Thora and Art's backyard and dreamed my sleeping baby was a boy with a fist of knotted muscle like my Dad's.

When I stopped in Rockville to try and find Art and Thora's house again, I found Stan, the adopted baby, now fifty years old, fixing up the old place. The hills spilled down into the backyard like waves that will never go, and as I remember it, the boulder was gray and brown, the hills red.

"You know your grandpa and his friend Art DeMille surveyed the road through Zion Park?"

Uncle Stan handed me a beer as I nodded.

"Yep, they were hired by the U.S. government." He continued, "Once the route was settled on, the job they'd been hired to do was done. So they got the bright idea of renting all the horses and wagons in Rockville, speculating that they would be needed in building the road. Their plan was to sublet them back to the government for a profit. Pretty smart?"

"It sounds like they were good business partners."

"They were more than partners. They were friends. Why, Art even married Dave's sister."

He told me how my Grandma Rosalie had left him, her newborn, with Thora and Art to raise, and departed for Idaho. It was hard traveling then, too hard maybe, for a new baby. So Stan grew up in Rockville away from the rest of his seven brothers and sisters, chased the trails and hunted the sunsets that my father, his big brother, chased and hunted until he was ten.

Corey, maybe I'll spend this summer there in Rockville, if I can, and see if by glancing over my shoulder at the past I can, once again, find my father, or something of myself, at least. Or perhaps gain some glimpse of my grandfather, David Alma, never known. Then if some storm should arise, I'll be protected, anchored by the past.

I've often wondered if my grandfather, this lost progenitor, this precursor of self, felt any of the things I feel? Was he lost among his many brothers and sisters? What had been bonded between Art and him that Rosalie, his wife, should gift it with a son? Why do I come circling around, wondering? And his nine children, were they consolation enough for life's flaws?

Stan told me, "Dave and Art were friends," and looked sideways at me.

Devoted to an existence that is largely poetic, some phraseless melody whispers between the walls of my room, as I consider this: My past is my estate, and my companions are conjecture and imagination, but are they concrete enough to give me dimension, like the stone in my Great Aunt Thora's backyard—the place where my father leaned, and played, while his father watched.

He had the most majestic face, my father's father. It was almost classic in profile. I have a picture of him sitting astride a horse when he was fourteen or fifteen years old. His spine is ramrod straight, supporting a melancholy face, like all photographs in those days. He could be a double of his grandson, my brother, Jerry, born the day he died twenty-eight years later.

Rosalie once remarked to her grown children, "If he hadn't been my husband I would have been in love with him myself. He was a ladies' man. The pumpkin in the patch."

In school play Grandma once saw me do, she told me I 'showed leg' just the way grandpa had. It was strange to hear I looked like someone I had never known.

Did his friend Art make him smile? Were they buddies in Rockville? Did they go swimming and admire each other's bodies in the sun? Did they drink from the same stream and wash each others hands and necks? Did Rosalie weep to leave the baby behind?

So Corey, the Bit and Spur lies directly on the route that my grandfather and his friend took into the canyon each day to go to work.

Death drops our bodies away to affirm we have a soul. Did Art have a premonition the day grandpa was killed? Did he lean his sunburned arm against the cab window of Dave's pickup and smile, trying to memorize the curve of his friend's brow? Did the sun set a halo behind Art's head as he leaned there? Did he have some urge to say to his friend, "Don't go!"? How had winter been that year?

Did Rosalie stop short while taking care of house, wondering what was amiss? Did Art find the truck and carry Dave's broken body back up to the road? Did he carry the news to Rosalie? Did Rosalie leave shortly after the accident, for Idaho, in order to be settled into the new land before summer peaked?

All year long I'll keep a plant, a fern or some day lilies, sitting on my gas heater. Invariably, one cold day I'll turn on the heat and fry these plants. In my absentmindedness, forgetting they had been basking there in the window light. I can easily imagine the plant screams sent into the evening air.

There is a cyclical action that takes place in my heart, periodic mood swings that seem to repeat themselves. As if there is a silent alarm and plant screams go off in my head, forerunner to Jekyll-like convolutions in behavior. I yearn for emotional constancy. How do people do it? I often find myself staring at couples. Hoping that by watching them I may be able to learn secrets about their behavior.

My fevers still come and go. Flashing hot and cold, I'll sometimes sleep until three in the afternoon on weekends, then I'll catch the bus and ride to the end of the line and back again for no reason. Hypnotized by the heat and the rhythm, lately I'll have flashes of my father/grandfather standing in the dust of the field with his hand on his hip, leaning against a tractor. His hat is shading his eyes. I look for an echo of him in my lovers, that man leaning on the tractor. I see him now, moving through the fields wearing big irrigation boots, long-handled shovel over his shoulder. In the sunset his hair is like rusting iron.

Would he be glad to know I look for an echo of him in the men I meet? It was my father I saw in you, Corey. I never knew that until he died. Maybe that's why my thoughts have been filled with him and you these days. Maybe that's why I'm writing.

I know it isn't over yet, what passed between my father and me. Death can end a life, but it does not end a relationship. I still remember him, and I write these words in praise of him. He'll always be a key figure in my personal mythos. He is me. I am a side of him—his offspring, his son.

He was much closer in lifestyle to his father, by far, than I was to him. They both remained connected to the earth throughout their lives. I burn day lilies on my gas heater. He was not my friend and he did not understand me, though I did come to love him. Was it so between him and his father?

I still remember what he said to me after they took you away, after he figured out what had passed between the two of us.

"These things are wrong."

He said it again shortly before he died, "The things you are doing are wrong."

What would you have me do, Dad? Go through life alone? I don't desire women the way I do men. What would you have me do?

❀

At night I dream of having no sons and wake weeping for my children because they are not.

❀

Death can end a life, but I still have that same conversation with him over and over and over, and yet still I see that man shading his eyes, moving through the fields, irrigation boots whispering and clumping through the long grass. I follow behind. Sometimes he turns and it's you, Corey, sometimes my dad. Do you want to hear these things? I wonder.

Ah, Corey, where are you? What are you doing? What has happened? Do you think of me as often as I think of you? Did we come together so intensely only to turn and go our separate ways? Was it just circumstance? Didn't we have any say in the matter?

Imagine a world where no one told us what we were supposed to be, or they just forgot somehow, and we got to invent ourselves fresh from the beginning. It seems the one thing that we should have been taught—how to love—was ignored and so now the only thing I can feel is desire, and it is for other men. I guess because I somehow imagine another man will understand this loneliness I feel and I hope, futilely I fear, sympathy will turn into love.

🏵

Perhaps one day, in the midst of one of my fevers, I'll see a man leaning, hat shading his eyes, and he will beckon to me to come near. (Perhaps this summer in Springdale, Corey.) I'll go and stand next to him. The plant screams will stop ringing in my head and my fevers will go away. The dimming of the stars will find us sleeping and perhaps the shadow of my father will pause at our door and glance benevolence toward us.

New American Fiction Series
Published by Sun & Moon Press

Winer of the Carey-Thomas Award for the
Best Example of Creative Publishing (1987)

1. WIER & POUCE, Steve Katz ($16.95, $10.95)
2. MANGLED HANDS, Johnny Stanton ($15.95, $10.95)
3. NEW JERUSALEM, Len Jenkin ($10.95)
4. CITY OF GLASS, Paul Auster ($13.95)
5. GHOSTS, Paul Auster ($12.95)
6. THE LOCKED ROOM, Paul Auster ($13.95)
7. BLOWN AWAY, Ronald Sukernick ($16.95, $10.95)
8. THE MEMOIRS OF THE LATE MR. ASHLEY, Marianne Hauser ($11.95)
9. COUNTRY COUSINS, Michael Brownstein ($11.95)
10. FLORRY OF WASHINGTON HEIGHTS, Steve Katz ($15.95, $10.95)
11. DREAD, Robert Steiner ($15.95, $10.95)
12. FAMILY LIFE, Russell Banks ($15.95)
13. PAINTED TURTLE: WOMAN WITH GUITAR, Clarence Major ($14.95)
14. THE SEA-RABBIT, Wendy Walker ($16.95, $11.95)
15. THE DEEP NORTH, Fanny Howe (paperback, Sun & Moon Classics: 15) ($9.95)
16. HOTEL DEATH AND OTHER TALES, John Perreault ($16.95, $10.95)
17. MUSIC FROM THE EVENING OF THE WORLD, Michael Brownstein ($15.95, $10.95)
18. METAPHYSICS IN THE MIDWEST, Curtis White ($15.95, $10.95)
19. THE RED ADAM, Mark Mirsky ($10.95)
20. A FREE MAN, Lewis Warsh ($12.95)
21. THE PETRUS BOREL STORIES, Welch Everman ($12.95)
22. THE FORTUNETELLER, Mac Wellman ($11.95)
23. TAR BEACH, Richard Elman ($12.95)
24. THE HARRY AND SYLVIA STORIES, Welch Everman ($12.95)
25. THE PRICE OF ADMISSION, San Eisenstein ($12.95)
26. THE CRIMSON BEARS, Tom LaFarge ($13.95)
27. THE IDEA OF HOME, Curtis White ($12.95)
28. MY HORSE AND OTHER STORIES, Stacey Levine ($11.95)
29. THE SONS OF XAVIER KEEP MARCHING, Johnny Stanton ($13.95)